The Hawk Is Hungry

Volume 22

SUN TRACKS
An American Indian Literary Series

Series Editors
Larry Evers and Ofelia Zepeda

Editorial Committee
Vine Deloria, Jr.
Joy Harjo
N. Scott Momaday
Emory Sekaquaptewa
Leslie Marmon Silko

D'Arcy McNickle

The Hawk Is Hungry

& OTHER STORIES

Edited by Birgit Hans

University of Arizona Press

Tucson & London

Royalties from the sale of this book will be donated to the D'Arcy McNickle Center for the History of the American Indian at the Newberry Library, Chicago, Illinois.

The University of Arizona Press
Copyright © 1992
Arizona Board of Regents

⊖ This book is printed on acid-free, archival-quality paper.
Manufactured in the United States of America

97 96 95 94 93 92   6 5 4 3 2 1
LIBRARY OF CONGRESS CATALOGING-IN-PUBLICATION DATA
McNickle, D'Arcy, 1904–1977.
    The hawk is hungry and other stories /
  D'Arcy McNickle ; Birgit Hans, editor.
      p. cm. — (Sun tracks ; v. 22)
    Includes bibliographical references.
    ISBN 0-8165-1326-0 (alk. paper). —
    ISBN 0-8165-1331-7 (pbk. : alk. paper)
    1. Indians of North America—Fiction.
    I. Hans, Birgit, 1957–   .
    II. Title. III. Series.
    PS3525.A2844H38   1992   92-8623
    813'.52—dc20   CIP
British Library Cataloguing-in-Publication Data
A catalogue record for this book is available from the British Library.

Contents

Acknowledgments   vi
Introduction   vii

THE RESERVATION
Hard Riding   3
En roulant ma boule, roulant . . .   13
Meat for God   25
Snowfall   35
Train Time   47

MONTANA
The Hawk Is Hungry   55
Debt of Gratitude   65
The Wedding Night   75
Newcomers   87
Man's Work   97
Going to School   107

THE CITY
Manhattan Wedlock   119
Let the War Be Fought   135
In the Alien Corn   145
Six Beautiful in Paris   161
The Silver Locket   165

Notes   173

Acknowledgments

I would like to express my gratitude to Larry Evers, who encouraged and helped me throughout the process, and to Antoinette McNickle Vogel, who was generous with her time and provided many insights into her father's character. I would also like to thank The Newberry Library in Chicago for permission to publish D'Arcy McNickle's unpublished short fiction. *Esquire* and *Common Ground* kindly granted permission to reprint "Meat for God" and "Snowfall" in this collection of McNickle's short fiction.

Introduction

*To have been born an Indian on an Indian
Reservation is to have been half-born. Rather, it is
to have come to live in a world of mist. Always you
are waiting, the people around you are waiting.*[1]

D'Arcy McNickle (1904–1977) began his literary career in the early
1930s during the Great Depression. A native of Montana and a
member of the Salish Kootenai Confederated Tribes, McNickle
wrote starkly realistic fiction depicting hard rural lives on farms,
ranches, and American Indian reservations in the American West.
In a few short stories he also explored urban lives set in such cities as
New York and Paris.

Although McNickle's novel *The Surrounded* (1936) is now widely
regarded as a classic fictional statement of American Indian life
during this period, his short fiction remains almost unknown; the
majority of his stories have never been published. This collection
makes them available for the first time.

What McNickle created in these short stories is a remarkable
portrait of the Depression-era West. The fictionalized place of his
work was not a popular one for Eastern readers conditioned by
such romantic renderings as Owen Wister's *The Virginian* (1901)
and Oliver La Farge's *Laughing Boy* (1930). McNickle himself once
stated, "I am writing of the West, not of the Indians primarily, and
certainly not of the romantic West which the best-selling authors
have exploited to the detriment of a rational understanding."[2] Mc-
Nickle instead echoes the sensibility of such varied Western realists as

Hamlin Garland, Ole Rolvaag, and Willa Cather in his work. Like theirs McNickle's region is a hard and unforgiving place that shatters the romantic expectations his characters bring to it. But one factor that sets McNickle's realistic perspective of the West apart is his understanding of himself as an American Indian. This understanding was gradual and hard won; in fact, it was acquired during the very years when these short stories were written.

THE MAN

William D'Arcy McNickle was born on January 14, 1904, in St. Ignatius, Montana. His father, William McNickle, the son of Irish immigrants, was a farmer and an industrial arts teacher. D'Arcy McNickle inherited his one-quarter Indian blood from his mother, Philomene Parenteau, whose ancestors were Métis, French Cree from the Duck Lake area of Saskatchewan, Canada.

McNickle's grandfather Isidore Parenteau was a close associate of the Métis leader Louis Riel.[3] During the second, failed Métis uprising in 1885, Parenteau barely managed to escape to Montana. He returned to Duck Lake after the Canadian government granted him amnesty in 1910, but Philomene grew up in Montana, separated from her Cree tribal roots. D'Arcy McNickle never established ties with his Cree relatives and considered himself Salish throughout his life.

In 1905, the year after McNickle's birth, Philomene presented herself and her three children, D'Arcy and his two older sisters Ruth and Florence, for adoption into the Salish Kootenai Confederated Tribes, also known as the Flathead.[4] This adoption made her and the children eligible to be deeded individual portions of the Flathead tribal lands in Montana. Philomene and her husband made use of the General Allotment Act of 1887, also known as the Dawes Act, in which the federal government provided for individual ownership of tribal lands. Philomene and her non-Indian husband William, whom she had married in 1899, were thereby able to establish a home.

The early years of D'Arcy McNickle's life must have been fraught with insecurities about his identity. His mother was a Métis who chose to become a Flathead Indian. Her marriage to a white man during this period of powerful assimilationist sentiment caused additional pressure. In a strongly autobiographical early draft of his first novel, *The Surrounded* (1936), the protagonist's white father describes mixed-blood marriages on the Flathead Reservation: "Wives were makeshift too. A white man married a squaw in the same way that he put dirt on the roof of his cabin in place of shingles. That was how he married a squaw. A squaw was all right until she gave you a child. There he lay in front of you, ugly and black. What could you do? Give him the best Christian name you could think of and let it go at that."[5] Listening to such views of white/Indian marriages may well have been a daily reality for D'Arcy McNickle as he grew up. Even at age seventy, McNickle remembered the uncertain, troubled days of his childhood: "My recollection of that period of my life is that we knew so little and tried to ignore what we did know, since it was not a source of pride. As 'breeds' we could not turn for reassurance to an Indian tradition and certainly not to the white community."[6]

The single most traumatic event of McNickle's childhood took place in 1914 when his parents divorced. The struggle between the mixed-blood mother and the white father for custody of their children and control of their land allotments was acrimonious. The dispute carried from Montana as far as the office of the Commissioner of Indian Affairs in Washington, D.C. In an effort to keep her children, Philomene wrote to the Commissioner that she had tried to "raise [D'Arcy] as white man, and fit him for a better lot in life, than the common indian."[7] At the end of the custody battle, William McNickle was given continued use of the children's allotted land. All three children were removed from the Flathead Reservation, where they were attending mission school, and sent to Chemawa, an Indian boarding school in Oregon.

Much later in his life McNickle commented on the purpose of boarding schools such as Chemawa in a nonfiction study he coauthored with Harold Fey, *Indians and Other Americans*. The general and distanced nature of his statement seems to indicate that it also represented his own experience: "Moreover, the schools were dedicated to the ultimate eradication of all traits of Indian culture. . . . If the child could be taken young enough away from the influences of family and tribe, the odds against his ever becoming a part of his environment were considered remote."[8] McNickle's mother had tried to "raise him as white man" and Chemawa continued on the same path.

McNickle returned from Chemawa Boarding School in 1917 and, at his mother's urging, took the name of her new white husband, Dahlberg.[9] The name change signaled a movement away from "the influences of family and tribe" during this period of his life, a movement that was stimulated by his reeducation at Chemawa.

In 1921, D'Arcy McNickle enrolled in the University of Montana, eventually pursuing a program in English literature and creative writing. Encouraged by his professors, he began to write short fiction and poetry and published some work in the *Frontier and Midland,* a literary journal published by the University of Montana. Published work from this period includes poems and such short fiction as "The Silver Locket" and "Going to School," both included in this collection.

At the suggestion of his professors, D'Arcy McNickle left Montana in 1925 to study at Oxford University in England for a year. Ironically, he financed this and additional travel in Europe by selling his land allotment on the Flathead Reservation, thereby weakening his ancestral ties even further. McNickle had left the University of Montana with the hope of completing his course work for an undergraduate degree at Oxford. Unfortunately, that proved impossible, but what he did take away from Oxford was as important to him throughout his life as a degree would have been: an increased awareness of the subtleties of the English language. His deliberate and extremely effective use of English was mentioned as early as 1936 in a review of *The Surrounded* and often in subsequent discussions of his work. McNickle never completed his university degree, but in 1966 the University of Colorado officially recognized his scholarly accomplishment by conferring an honorary doctorate on him.

By 1927 D'Arcy McNickle had settled in New York City, where he continued to live until 1935 and where he married Joran Birkeland, a fellow student at the University of Montana, who had accompanied him on his European travels. It was during these New York years that McNickle seems to have been most absorbed in his chosen work as a writer. And it was during these New York years that he experienced profound personal changes that shaped the remainder of his career.

The most visible of these changes occurred in 1933 when, on the occasion of the birth of his elder daughter Antoinette, he gave up the name of his stepfather, Dahlberg, and became D'Arcy McNickle once again. The name change is a sign of a more subtle change that took hold of McNickle during this time, a change that led to a new regard for his tribal heritage and a new commitment to it. He no longer denied either his growing up on the Flathead Reservation or his mixed-blood heritage. In fact, McNickle was prepared to explore the values of traditional Indian culture rather than to simply deny them as he had in early drafts of his first novel.

Clearly D'Arcy McNickle went to Europe, then settled in New York City, in order to distance himself from his rural Montana heritage and the bitter memories of his childhood. But it is equally evident that McNickle was also drawn by what he could learn as a writer only in such literary centers as London, Paris, and New York. Daily participation in the bustling life of the city excited and challenged him. He initially wanted to immerse himself completely in the cosmopolitan life of New York City. His diaries of that time are full of political discussions, sporting events, and book reviews. In one entry he explains what motivated him to take part in city life: "As with Henry Adams, so with me it is a question of education. Through long repetition, I had been led to assume that only the political, the engineer-trained, the extrovert, the 'smart,' the supersalesman, had any chance or right to survive."[10]

McNickle knew that it was going to be difficult to establish himself as a professional writer in New York City. For a time he was able to earn enough to live by working for publishing houses and trade journals, reviewing and editing manuscripts. He was on the staff of the *Encyclopedia Britannica* from 1927 to 1928; he worked on trade journals for E. F. Houghton and Co. in Philadelphia in 1929; and he edited manuscripts for the *National Cyclopaedia of American Biography* in New York from 1929 to 1934.[11] In his spare time he worked on his novel *The Surrounded* and wrote short fiction.

Despite the rejection slips he accumulated for his stories during those years, he never despaired of publishing his fiction. In 1932 he wrote in his diary of a conversation he had had with his wife Joran: "The wine brought on some very frank talk between us and we discussed the probabilities of finding a publisher any time that might be classed the near future—scarcely any, we agreed. She questioned if I were not expecting too much, but I thought not."[12] Soon after this still-hopeful entry the Depression took hold and work became even more scarce.

The year 1934 proved to be a turning point in D'Arcy McNickle's life. In a letter written at the beginning of that year he first acknowledged his growing involvement in the historical and contemporary treatment of Native Americans: "My interest is that of one of the original Americans hounded into the earth who see, at last, the beginning of a wholly devoted and wholly sincere effort to recreate the glory that was in these Americas before the Christian barbarians came to impose a 'higher' civilization upon the innocent."[13] By 1934, D'Arcy McNickle had also decided to apply for work to the Bureau of Indian Affairs. Attracted to the innovative and reformist administration of John Collier, McNickle took a decisive step toward a recognition of himself as an American Indian and toward a commitment to the American Indian community he had left after college. In his application McNickle wrote, "I am a native of the Flathead Reservation in Montana, and I believe that the records there show me as a quarter breed. The Indian blood comes through my mother, who was really of Cree descent but was adopted by the Flathead tribe when her father settled in Western Montana, after having been expelled from Canada for having participated in the Riel Rebellion in 1885."[14]

From this time on D'Arcy McNickle worked tirelessly and successfully as an advocate for Native Americans as an administrator, as a scholar, as an educator, and as a writer. The list of his accomplishments is long. From 1936 to 1952 McNickle served as administrative assistant, as field representative, as assistant to the commissioner, and as Director of Tribal Relations in the Bureau of Indian Affairs. He was executive director of American Indian Development from 1959 to 1966, professor of Anthropology at the University of Saskatchewan, Regina Campus from 1966 to 1971, and Program Director for the Center for the History of the American Indian at The Newberry Library from 1972 to 1977. He was also a founding member of the National Congress of American Indians and he edited numerous books on the contemporary American Indian situation. His own work as a writer includes such studies as *They Came Here First: The Epic of the American Indian* (1949); *Indians and Other Americans* (1959), on which he collaborated with Harold E. Fey; *Native American Tribalism* (1962); and *Indian Man* (1971), a biography of Oliver La Farge. McNickle published two novels in addition to *The Surrounded: Runner in the Sun* (1954), a novel for young readers, and *Wind from an Enemy Sky,* which was published posthumously in 1978. That the prestigious Center for the Study of American Indian History at The Newberry Library has been named in D'Arcy McNickle's honor is indicative of the magnitude of his stature among both academic communities and American Indian communities.

McNickle was married three times. His first marriage to Joran Birkeland could not withstand the pressure of the Great Depression and broke up in 1936, shortly after their move to Washington, D.C. In the late 1930s McNickle married Roma Kauffman and his second daughter Kathleen was born in 1940. Divorced in 1967, McNickle married his third wife, the sociologist Viola Pfrommer, in 1969. Tragically, she developed Alzheimer's disease at the beginning of the 1970s and died in 1977, a few months before McNickle himself died of a massive coronary on October 18.

Despite his growing national acclaim after 1936, McNickle remained an intensely private man. Alfonso Ortiz, a long-time friend, says of McNickle the man, "Those of us who felt befriended by this very strong and private man may recall the equally private gifts he bestowed upon us, each in our turn. . . . He always led the way but, as a true friend he never intruded himself on the privacy of his companions' perception and experience. He did not so much charge these special places with his own meanings as he pointed to older meanings already inherent in them."[15]

THE STORIES

It is impossible to date precisely the majority of D'Arcy McNickle's short stories. Of the sixteen stories included in this collection, only six have been published, as far as I could determine. The other ten stories exist in manuscript among the papers McNickle left to The Newberry Library in Chicago. The diaries that McNickle kept indicate that most of his short fiction was written during the years he lived in New York City, 1927–1935. These were essentially the same years when he was producing a series of drafts of *The Surrounded,* and the same years when he was moving increasingly toward identifying himself as an American Indian.

Lacking any reliable way to date the stories, I have opted to present them thematically rather than chronologically. The three themes are the Reservation, Montana, and the City. This arrangement, I believe, reflects the importance of place in McNickle's short fiction. The stories in the Reservation and Montana sections are McNickle's answer both to the popular romantic literature of the West and to the stereotyped historical accounts of the West.

McNickle's primary interest, however, was in people and "the character which was formed by the impact of the Frontier upon the lives of the people who settled it,"[16] and not in history. The basic theme of his short stories concerns the community and the outsider or the individual within the community who infringes upon its traditions. In these stories the community usually manages to maintain its traditions and to survive. McNickle's short stories also explore the relationship of the community and individuals with the landscape in which they live; if they cannot come to terms with their environment, they deteriorate, since they also lose the support of the community that the environment sustains. McNickle explores this theme very poignantly in the stories set in the city. His growing disillusionment with the city is shown in short stories, early drafts of *The Surrounded,* and entries in his diaries, in which he sets the city in opposition to a country frequently associated with his native Montana.

The stories will be of special interest to those who have read McNickle's masterwork, *The Surrounded,* since McNickle continues to deal with many of the themes evident in the novel. He merely broadens the focus; in his short fiction these themes are regarded as universal rather than specific for the mixed-blood and full-blood Indian caught between two cultures. The stories will also be of interest to those who seek greater understanding of the life of one of the most important American Indian leaders of the 20th century.

The best of D'Arcy McNickle's short stories, however, deserve an audience for their own merits.

McNickle's powerful short story "Hard Riding" takes the romance out of Cowboy-and-Indian fantasies of the West, just as the stories of the Montana farmers deflate the fantasy of creating an Edenic garden in the West. In "Hard Riding" McNickle explores the strength of a tribal community that manages to defend its values and traditions against Superintendent Brinder, a representative of the federal government's Indian Service. Superintendent Brinder embodies a collection of stereotypical beliefs about the American West and about American Indians. He regards Indians as no more than tools to accomplish his own personal dream of possessing a cattle empire: "He had a special liking for cattle. It began long before he had ever seen an Indian back home in New York State. Boyhood reading about hard riding and fast shooting on the cattle trails—that was what started it. Then in his first job in the Indian Service, he had worked under a hard-minded Scotchman whose record as a stockman was unbeatable. He had learned the gospel from him. He learned to talk the lingo." Brinder's dream exists only in such "lingo." He tries to speak the language and live the plot of a pulp western. The conflict he thinks he faces as a representative of the federal government is clear: a benevolent white man's struggle to bring civilization and material progress to lazy, mentally inferior Indians. Brinder does not take the Indians' reluctance to follow his plot seriously. Their final compliance, he believes, is inevitable. It has been plotted that way in the stereotypical westerns he has read.

But as McNickle makes clear, Brinder lacks the mental agility of his Indian charges, who will not be cajoled into giving up traditional tribal law, their means of survival as a people. In the classic role of a tribal trickster, Big Face manages to satisfy Brinder's demands to the letter without permitting the spirit of the demands to divide the Indian community: "It is better, we think, that fools should be judges. If people won't listen to them, no one will mind." Just such ironic reversals are the stock and trade of tricksters in Native American oral traditions, such as Coyote from the Salish Kootenai oral tradition. Many years later, almost at the end of his life, McNickle explained the importance of Coyote, the trickster, in a letter: "Indian story telling presents a contrasting view of man's role in historical process: the coyote tales are especially good for this. Coyote is rarely a hero, or if he starts out to be a hero invariably he ends up a scoundrel or he finds himself outsmarted. There are no mounting crises and no gratifying denouements. Life is an arrangement of reciprocal expectations and obligations, and no one is allowed to set himself up as a power unto himself."[17] McNickle's use of the trickster figure to deflate the ambitions of a Euro-American bureaucrat in "Hard Riding" anticipates brilliantly the use of tricksters in the work of such contemporary American Indian writers as N. Scott Momaday, Simon J. Ortiz, Leslie Silko, Gerald Vizenor, Louise Erdrich, and fellow Montanan James Welch.[18]

In "En roulant ma boule, roulant . . ." McNickle shifts to an exploration of a similar conflict within the reservation community. Here problems with governance and the law cannot be so easily laid at the feet of a bureaucratic fool like Brinder. Rather, McNickle explores the complex interactions between mixed-blood and full-blood Indians as they struggle with competing legal systems. Even though the mixed-blood judges talk vaguely of "English common law, the Napoleonic Code, Statutory law, Blackstone, Chancellor Kent" and the like, they cannot clearly grasp the concepts imposed on them by the Anglo-American legal system. At the same time, the opening scene shows that they have also lost the ability to summon concepts from their Indian heritage: "The judges stalled for time. Embarrassment and unconfessed ignorance snuffed out their wits. Four hundred years lay barren in them." The mixed-bloods' attempts to interpret another people's laws are doomed to failure. Even the spectators come with one expectation only, to be amused. Sam Delorme, the French and Cree father of the "raped" Pauline, is ridiculed and made into an example of the purposeless mixed-blood community. His only interest in life is food and even his appearance causes amusement: "his wide quarters hanging like over-running dough round the seat's edge."

Dieudonné, a representative of the full-blood community, makes it clear from the beginning that he merely tolerates the clumsy attempts of the mixed-bloods to judge him by a foreign law. The only law that he will submit to is the one that has grown with the country and the experience of his people. That native experience is embodied for him in the song of Le Premier, the tribal patriarch: "He had a vivid imagery of a song which went back into mistiness, like a living thread of water which you might watch from a grassy hill top inlaying its silvered course in the prairie and disappearing in a final gleam on the horizon's uncertain edge. So it was a song, *En roulant ma boule, roulant . . .* rather than a connected narrative, which he knew so intimately. Yet it was a song which gave him a full sense of the narrative." While the courtroom scene serves to awaken Dieudonné to this link with his own history, the ride to Le Premier's deathbed late in the story intensifies his realization. It emphasizes Dieudonné's importance as a favorite, perhaps a spiritual heir, of Le Premier. His very name, "Dieudonné"—God given—indicates that he may become a new custodian of tribal tradition and memory.

"The Hawk Is Hungry" is one of D'Arcy McNickle's best stories dealing with rural life in the West. McNickle describes attempts to farm the arid mountainous West in a way that is reminiscent of Hamlin Garland's *Main-Travelled Roads* (1891). McNickle shows the farmers' closeness to the soil but, at the same time, the futility of their attempts to get more than a minimal living from the land. Individuals are slowly destroyed through backbreaking labor. In the end the farmer becomes a slave to the land rather than being ennobled by his work on it.

In "The Hawk Is Hungry" two sisters who have been school teachers in the East move to the West in order to live out their pastoral dreams. They take up residence on an unproductive Montana farm, and there can scratch but the barest living from the land. Yet they refuse to give up their dreams of making a garden in the West, even when a pet hen is killed by a hawk: "That hen was an idea. The idea of personal integrity. Standing alone and damn the consequences. Men try to live like that. Few do. Very few. The hen did. Did you see her? And this hawk, he's a witless brute force that insults us all. The best of us! We put ourselves above the beast, but when the hawk is hungry he comes for us. And what are we then?" The sisters must admit to themselves for the first time that they are not in charge of their own destinies. Still, stubbornly, they cling to the dream of the West as a garden, an agricultural paradise.

The narrator's sister, Anne, a visitor to their farm from the East, takes a detached viewpoint that permits her to see the sisters' romantic notions for what they are: self-deception. Anne sums up the sisters' self-inflicted loss: "I wonder—was it worth it—if that's the way the West was settled?"

While the earlier drafts of *The Surrounded* and McNickle's early diary entries describe the city (be it New York or Paris) as an ideal place for the assimilation that the young McNickle desired for himself, the short stories set in the city show McNickle's growing disillusionment. A promising but unfinished short story, "Six Beautiful in Paris," for example, sets rural values against those of the city.

In "Six Beautiful in Paris," McNickle reunites two American brothers. They have not seen each other for more than twenty years. Waldo Verriman is an exquisitely mannered, calculating professor of romance literature, whose sophistication has made possible his acceptance into the intelligentsia of Paris, a society reputed to be the most civilized and liberal in the world. Unfortunately, Waldo Verriman's achievements have been at the cost of his humanity: His only thought at the unexpected reunion with his elder brother, Robert, is of the embarrassment Robert and his family may cause Waldo among his Paris friends.

Robert echoes some of the brash American characters in Henry James' novels, notably Christopher Newman in *The American*. He is a successful Montana rancher and is loud, unrefined, and very wealthy. Just like Waldo, Robert is always ready to talk about himself. He speaks of his money and Montana at every opportunity. Yet Robert shows a genuine concern for his family and for his brother.

The two brothers have achieved completely different kinds of success: one is defined by intellectual achievement and the other by material achievement. Both are satisfied with the life they have created for themselves. McNickle's perspective is clear, however. Urban life and the forms it imposes on those who live in the city destroy the more truly humane values of those from a rural background.

Stories such as "Six Beautiful in Paris" echo the earliest extant draft of *The Surrounded*, titled "The Hungry Generations," but unlike "In the Alien Corn," are not taken directly from the draft. The setting in the draft is not restricted to Montana as is that in the published version. "The Hungry Generations" has three distinct parts. Part one describes the mixed-blood Archilde's return to his father's ranch in order to say good-bye forever, his reluctant involvement with the work on the ranch and his family members who live there, the death of the game warden, his reconciliation with his father, and finally, his father's death. The first part of the published version covers the same incidents. Part two of "The Hungry Generations" covers Archilde's quest for education in Paris while *The Surrounded* has no such journey. In part three of "The Hungry Generations," Archilde runs his father's ranch, is jailed for the murder of the game warden, is exonerated in a trial, and accepted into white Montana society. This version does not go much beyond the assimilationist attitudes evident in the work of such early American Indian writers as John Milton Oskison and John Joseph Mathews.[19] While the plot develops along similar lines in the latter part of *The Surrounded,* Archilde's attitude toward his Indian heritage has changed completely. Instead of attempting to assimilate unconditionally into white Montana society, Archilde gains a new respect for the Flathead; he may be arrested for a crime he did not commit at the end of the novel, but he has come to terms with both his Indian and white blood.

The Archilde of "The Hungry Generations" journeys to Paris to find himself and to gain a sophistication like that of Waldo Verriman. Archilde does not succeed in Paris, though, and in this early draft leaves the bewildering city behind in order to return to rural Montana.

"In the Alien Corn" is another story in this collection that was originally a part of the early draft of *The Surrounded.* In this story McNickle again attempts to explore the effect of the city on people who have removed themselves from their rural roots in a desire to gain sophistication and artistic recognition. The consequence of the mother's single-minded struggle for her sons' fame is insanity; the city has removed her emotional ties to other family members and they therefore cannot fill the void caused by her sons' failure to fulfill her ambitions. The city is a site of disillusionment and despair. D'Arcy McNickle's use of the city in his work anticipates later treatment of

Indian relocation by such writers as N. Scott Momaday and Louise Erdrich.

McNickle's greatest contribution to American literature is undoubtedly *The Surrounded*, with its juxtaposed broken narratives used as structural devices and its oral traditions used as essential narrative elements. McNickle does not use these strategies to enrich the texture of his short stories, but he does manage to leave behind the "world of mist," the search for the expectations of the white world, and to start an exploration of self that was to culminate in the novel. The short stories of D'Arcy McNickle represent a crucial step in his life as a writer, as well as in his life as a politician and historian.

▷ ▷ ▷   THE RESERVATION

Hard Riding

▷ ▷ ▷   Riding his gray mare a hard gallop in the summer dust, Brinder Mather labored with thought which couldn't quite come into focus.

The horse labored too, its gait growing heavy as loose sand fouled its footing; but at each attempt to break stride into a trot, there was the prick of spur point, a jerk at the reins. It was a habit with the rider.

"Keep going! Earn your feed, you hammerhead!"

Brinder was always saying that his horses didn't earn their feed. Yet he was the hardest rider in the country.

Feeling as he did about horses, he quite naturally had doubts about Indians. And he had to work with Indians. He was their superintendent . . . a nurse to their helplessness, was the way he sometimes thought of it.

It was getting toward sundown. The eastward mirror of the sky reflected orange and crimson flame thwarting the prismatic heavens. It was after supper, after a hard day at the Agency office, and Brinder was anxious to get his task done and be home to rest. The heat of the day had fagged him. His focusing thought came out in words, audibly.

"They've been fooling with the idea for a month, more than a month, and I still can't tell what they'll do. Somehow I've got to put it over. Either put it over or drop it. I'll tell them that. Take it or leave it. . . ."

Ahead, another mile, he saw the white schoolhouse, the windows ablaze with the evening sun. He wondered if those he had called together would be there, if they would all be there. A full turn-out, he reasoned, would indicate that they were interested. He could be encouraged if he saw them all on hand.

As he drew nearer, he observed that a group stood waiting. He tried to estimate the number . . . twelve or fifteen. Others were still coming. There were riders in the distance coming by other roads. The frown relaxed on his heavy, sun-reddened face. For the moment he was satisfied. He had called the entire Tribal Council of twenty, and evidently they would all be on hand. Good!

He let his horse slow to less than a canter for the first time in the three-mile ride from the Agency.

$$\nabla$$

"Hello, boys. Everybody coming tonight? Let's go inside."

He strode, tall and dignified, through the group.

They smiled to his words, saying nothing. One by one they followed him into the schoolroom. He was always for starting things with a rush; they always hung back. It was a familiar pattern. He walked to the teacher's desk and spread out before him a sheaf of paper which he had brought in a heavy envelope.

In five years one got to know something about Indians. Even in one's first job as superintendent of a Reservation, five years was a good schooling.

The important thing, the first thing to learn, was not to let them stall you. They would do it every time if you let them. They would say to a new idea, "Let us talk about that" or "Give us time. We'll think about it." One had to know when to cut short. Put it over or drop it. Take it or leave it.

Not realizing that at the start, he had let these crazy Mountain Indians stall on him a long time before he had begun to get results. He had come to them with a simple idea and only now, after five years, was it beginning to work.

Cattle . . . that was the idea. Beef cattle. Blooded stock. Good bulls. Fall round-ups. The shipment East. Cash profits. In language as simple as that he had finally got them to see his point. He had a special liking for cattle. It began long before he had ever seen an Indian, back home in New York State. Boyhood reading about hard riding and fast shooting on the cattle trails . . . that was what started it. Then, in his first job in the Indian Service, he had worked under a hard-minded Scotchman whose record as a stockman was unbeatable. He had learned the gospel from him. He learned to talk the lingo.

"Indians don't know, more than that don't give a damn, about dragging their feet behind a plow. Don't say as I blame 'em. But Indians'll always ride horses. They're born to that. And if they're going to ride horses they might as well be riding herd on a bunch of steers. It pays money."

He put it that way, following his Scotch preceptor. He put it to the Indians, to Washington officials, and to anybody he could buttonhole for a few minutes. It was a complete gospel. It was appropriations of money from Congress for cattle purchases. It won flattering remarks from certain visitors who were always around inquiring about Indian welfare. In time, it won over the Indians. It should have won them sooner.

The point was just that, not to let them stall on you. After five years he had learned his lesson. Put it over, or drop it.

He had taken off his broad-brimmed cattleman's hat and laid it on the desk beside his papers. The hat was part of the creed. He surveyed the score of wordless, pensive, buckskin-smelling Indians, some slouched forward, holding their big hats between their knees; others, hats on, silently smoking.

He had to put it across, this thing he wanted them to do. He had to do it now, tonight, or else drop it. That was what he had concluded.

"I think you fellows have learned a lot since I been with you. I appreciate the way you co-operate with me. Sometimes it's kinda hard to make things clear, but once you see what it means to you, you're all for it. I like that." He paused and mopped his brow. The schoolroom was an oven. The meeting should have been held outside—but never mind.

"In our stock association, we run our cattle together on a common range. We share the costs of riding range, rounding up, branding, and buying breeding bulls. Every time you sell a steer you pay a five-dollar fee into the pot, and that's what pays the bills. That's one of the things I had to tell you about. You didn't understand at first, but once you did, you went ahead. Today, it's paying dividends.

"You never had as much cash profit in your life before. Your steers are better beef animals, because the breeding is better. We got the class in bulls. And you get better prices because you can dicker with the buyers. But you know all that. I'm just reminding you."

Someone coughed in the back of the room and Brinder, always on guard, like the cowboys contending with rustlers and sheepmen he used to read about, straightened his back and looked sharply. But it was only a cough, repeated several times—an irritating, ineffective kind of cigarette cough. No one else in the audience made a sound. All were held in the spell of Brinder's words, or at any rate were waiting for him to finish what he had to say.

"We have one bad defect yet. You know what I mean, but I'll mention it just the same. In other words, fellows, we all of us know that every year a certain number of cattle disappear. The wolves don't get them and they don't die of natural causes. They are always strong, fat, two- or three-year-old steers that disappear, the kind that wolves don't monkey with and that don't die naturally. I ain't pointing my finger at anybody, but you know as well's I do that there's a certain element on the Reservation that don't deserve fresh meat, but always has it. They're too lazy or too ornery or they just don't know what it's all about. But they get fresh meat just the same.

"I want you fellows to get this. Let it sink in deep. Every time a fat steer goes to feed some Slick Steve too lazy to earn his keep, some of you are out around seventy-five, eighty dollars. You lose that much. Ponder that, you fellows."

He rustled the papers on the desk, looking for a row of figures: number of beef animals lost in five years (estimated), their money value, in round numbers. He hurled his figures at them, cudgeling.

"Some of you don't mind the loss. Because it's poor people getting the meat. It keeps someone from starving. That's what you say. What I say is—that ain't a proper way to look at it. First of all, because it's stealing and we can't go to countenancing stealing, putting up with it, I mean. Nobody has to starve, remember that. If you want to do something on your own book for the old people who can't work, you can. You can do what you like with your money. But lazy people, these Slick Steves who wouldn't work on a bet, nobody should give it easy to them, that's what I'm saying."

He waited a moment, letting the words find their way home. "There's a solution, as I told you last month. We want to set up a court, a court of Indian judges, and you will deal with these fellows in your own way. Give a few of them six months in jail to think it over, and times will begin to change around here. . . ."

That was the very point he had reached the last time he talked to the Council, a month before. He had gone no further, then, because they had begun asking questions, and from their questions he had discovered that they hadn't the least idea what he was driving at. Or so they made it appear. "If we have a tribal court," somebody would ask, "do we have to put somebody in jail?" That, obviously, was intentionally naive. It was intended to stall him off. Or some old man would say: "If somebody has to go to jail, let the Superintendent do it. Why should we have to start putting our own people in jail?" Such nonsense as that had been talked.

Finally, the perennial question of money came up. Would the Government pay for the court? A treacherous question, and he had answered without flinching.

"That's another thing," he had said brightly. "We're going to get away from the idea of the Government paying for everything. Having your own business this way, making a profit from it, you can pay for this yourselves. That will make you independent. It will be your own court, not the Government's court, not the Superintendent's court. No. The court will be supported by the fee money you pay when you sell a steer.

That speech broke up the meeting. It was greeted by a confusion of talk in the native tongue which gradually subsided in form of one speaker, one of the ancients, who obviously was a respected leader. Afterwards, a young, English-speaking tribesman translated.

"The old man here, Looking Glass, says the Gover'ment don't give us nothing for nothing. The money it spends on us, that's our own money, he says. It belongs to us and they keep it there at Washington, and nobody can say how much it is or how much has been lost. He says, where is all that money that they can't afford to pay for this court? That's what he says."

There was the snare which tripped up most Agency plans, scratch an old Indian, and the reaction was always the same. "Where's the money the Government owes us? Where's our land? Where's our treaty?" They were like a whistle with only one stop, those old fellows. Their tune was invariable, relentless and shrill. That was why one dreaded holding a meeting when the old men were present. Now the young fellows, who understood Agency plans. . . .

Anyhow, here he was trying it again, going over the plan with great care and patience. Much of the misunderstanding had been ironed out in the meantime. So he had been led to believe.

"This court will put an end to all this trouble," he was going on, trying to gauge the effect of his words, watching for a reaction. At last it came. One of the old men was getting to his feet.

He was a small man, emaciated by age and thin living, yet neat looking. His old wife, obviously, took good care of his clothes, sewed buckskin patches on his overalls and kept him in new moccasins. He talked firmly, yet softly, and not for very long. He sat down as soon as he had finished and let the interpreter translate for him.

"The old man here, Big Face, says the court, maybe, is all right. They have talked it over among themselves, and maybe it's all right. Our agent, he says, is a good man. He rides too fast. He talks too fast. But he has a good heart, so maybe the court is all right. That's what Big Face says."

The words were good, and Brinder caught himself smiling, which was bad practice when dealing with the old fellows. They were masters at laying traps for the unwary—that, too, he had learned in five years. Their own expressions never changed, once they got going, and you could never tell what might be in their minds.

Just the same, he felt easier. Big Face, the most argumentative of the lot, had come around to accept this new idea, and that was something gained. The month had not been lost.

He had something more to say. He was getting to his feet again, giving a tug to his belt and looking around, as if to make sure of his following. He had been appointed spokesman. That much was clear.

He made a somewhat longer speech, in which he seemed to express agitation, perhaps uncertainty. One could never be sure of tone values. Sometimes the most excitable sounding passages of this strange tongue were very tame in English. Brinder had stopped smiling and waited for the translation.

"Big Face here says there's only one thing they can't decide about. That's about judges. Nobody wants to be a judge. That's what they don't like. Maybe the court is all right, but nobody wants to be judge."

Brinder was rather stumped by that. He rose to his feet, quickly, giving everyone a sharp glance. Was this the trap?

"Tell the old man I don't understand that. It is an honor, being a judge. People pay money to be a judge in some places. Tell Big Face I don't understand his objection."

The old man was on his feet as soon as the words had been translated for him.

"It's like this. To be a judge, you got to be about perfect. You got to know everything, and you got to live up to it. Otherwise, you got nothing to say to anybody who does wrong. Anybody who puts himself up to be that good, he's just a liar. And people will laugh at him. We are friends among ourselves and nobody interferes in another person's business. That's how it is, and nobody wants to set himself up and be a judge. That's what Big Face says."

There it was—as neatly contrived a little pitfall as he had ever seen. He had to admire it—all the time letting himself get furious. Not that he let them see it. No, in five years, he had learned that much. Keep your head, and when in doubt, talk your head off. He drew a deep breath and plunged into an explanation of all the things he had already explained, reminding them of the money they lost each year, of the worthless fellows who were making an easy living from their efforts, of the proper way to deal with the problem. He repeated all the arguments and threw in as many more as he could think of.

"You have decided all this. You agree the court is a good thing. But how can you have a court without judges? It's the judges that make a court."

He couldn't tell whether he was getting anywhere or not—in all likelihood, not. They were talking all together once more and it didn't look as if they were paying much attention to him. He waited.

"What's it all about?" he finally asked the interpreter, a young mixed-blood, who was usually pretty good about telling Brinder which way the wind of thought blew among the old people.

"I can't make out," the interpreter murmured, drawing closer to Brinder. "They are saying lots of things. But I think they're going to decide on the judges—they've got some kind of plan—watch out for it—now, one of the old men will speak."

It was Big Face raising to his feet once more. Looking smaller, more wizened than ever. The blurring twilight of the room absorbed some of his substance and made Brinder feel that he was losing his grip on the situation. A shadow is a difficult adversary and Big Face was rapidly turning into one.

"The agent wants this court. He thinks it's a good thing. So we have talked some more—and we agree. We will have this court." He paused briefly, allowing Brinder only a moment's bewilderment.

"Only we couldn't decide who would be judge. Some said this one, some said that one. It was hard. . . ."

Brinder coughed. "Have you decided on any one, Big Face?" He no longer knew which way things were drifting but only hoped for the best.

The old fellow's eyes, misted by age, actually twinkled. In the body of councillors somebody laughed and coughed in the same breath. Feet stirred and bodies shifted. Something was in the air. Haltingly, Big Face named the men—the most amazing trio the Reservation had to offer.

"Walks-in-the-Ground—Jacob Gopher—Twisted Horn . . ."

In the silence that followed, Brinder tried hard to believe he had heard the wrong names. A mistake had been made. It was impossible to take it seriously. These three men—no, it was impossible! The first, an aged imbecile dripping saliva—ready to die! The second, stone deaf and blind! The third, an utter fool, a half-witted clown, to whom no one listened.

"You mean this?" Brinder still could not see the full situation, but was afraid that the strategy was deliberate and final.

"Those will be the judges of this court," Big Face replied, smiling in his usual friendly way.

"But these men can't be judges! They are too old, or else too foolish. No one will listen to them . . ." Brinder broke off short. He saw that he had stated the strategy of the old men especially as they had intended it. His friendliness withered away.

Big Face did not hesitate, did not break off smiling. "It is better, we think, that fools should be judges. If people won't listen to them, no one will mind."

Brinder had nothing to say, not just then. He let the front legs of his chair drop to the floor, picked up his hat. His face had paled. After five years—still to let this happen. . . . Using great effort, he turned it off as a joke. "Boys, you should of elected me judge to your kangaroo court. I would have made a crackerjack."

The Indians laughed and didn't know what he meant, not exactly. But maybe he was right.

En roulant ma boule, roulant . . .

▷ ▷ ▷   It was four hundred years emerging in a piddle. So you might say. And Dieudonné Leroux, eighteen years old, could whiff it and taste it.

Four hundred years or more, beginning on the Newfoundland cod banks, and now it was 1925, and Dieudonné was undergoing a major operation performed by untaught backwoodsmen using pieces of broken glass, pitchforks and canthooks as instruments.

And between the codfishing to feed a pious Europe and the miserable little joke played on a boy who was liked by the girls, there lay forest and water trails leading into an empire of fur and lumber and minerals, trails laid by cruciferrant priests, trails built by trade and by a race's apologists. Forest and river and naked savages all passed under the steamroller. And here was Dieudonné, standing red-faced and angry. He knew the ways of the world better than did the mentally tattered and physically ragged half-bloods who sat on trial on him; and knowing that he knew better than they, they were enjoying putting the spurs to him.

Roll along, my ball! Roll on . . .

Sam Delorme, French and Cree, and fat, stood up and bellowed his complaint. He was coatless, since it was a hot June day, and his soft stomach bulged over the faded sash which girthed his shabby trousers about. Oily moisture shone on his dark skin. His shirt opened on a tangled gray mat of hairiness. He was hatless and breathless.

"—so I'm saying this good-for-nothing kid here, he ruined my little Pauline."

Sam slumped into a chair, his wide quarters hanging like overrunning dough around the seat's edge.

Pauline did not look up at the conclusion of her father's words. But her face flushed. She was sentient.

There was a small square of cleared space near the front of the large room, with Pauline on one side and Dieudonné at the other. They faced a long table, and behind the table were the three "judges," in coatless undignity. Everywhere else in the room, sitting, standing, leaning and squatting, was the tightly packed audience, out of which came whispered comments and side bets. "How much that he did it?" The June heated room was smelly. Flies buzzed from face to face.

The judges stalled for time. Embarrassment and unconfessed ignorance snuffed out their wits. Four hundred years lay barren in them. So far they had spent most of their time arguing with the tribal policeman and among themselves, none quite daring to put the questions necessary to bring out the facts.

Steve Lame Boy, styled chief judge, strove with faint determination to lead the way through the maze, while his associates lent encouragement by poking him in the ribs. "Go it, Steve. You got to ask something, now." And he would try to shake them off. "Never mind. I'll ask something. Just shut up so I can get this straight."

He tried to browbeat the boy. "You, Dieudonné Leroux. Is that your name?"

The boy stood up in front of his chair—a boy not yet full grown. But he was all right. Yes, he would be all right, those near him were thinking. They studied him, as if he were a bull calf they were thinking of buying. Heavy shoulders, a good neck—it would fill out more; thick arms, too; hands rather long and thin, but strong perhaps; such was the scheme of him. An inch or two more of growth and he would be a man for anybody's measure. The men smiled, the women giggled, slyly. *Un homme, ça.* Let him fill out just a bit more, and he would be good meat. Nice face, too. Strong jaw, strong teeth, no doubt. Red lips, full. He would do.

"Is that your name, Dieudonné Leroux?" Steve Lame Boy repeated, his voice rising.

"Yes." The boy had gone from red to pale under the pressure of rising to meet the impact of eyes, but his voice was stout with anger.

At that point the policeman, Henry Twist, who was thin and gawky and watery-eyed, objected. He never agreed with Steve, the judge, and why should he, since Steve was his brother-in-law and was always running for office against him.

"This ain't the way you should do. First you should make the girl here stand up and say is it true what her old man claims. Then the boy can say whether he did it."

At that a four-cornered argument broke out between the three judges and the policeman in mixed French and Cree. In the twilight of their talk appeared [. . .], unaccountable star shells out of English common law, the Napoleonic code, Statutory law, Blackstone, Chancellor Kent. . . .

Dieudonné, wearying, sat down. He had not looked at the girl Pauline since she had come in half-an-hour before. Evidently he had no intention of looking at her. Evidently she meant nothing to him. He stared angrily beyond the judges at the leafy tree showing through the window. The June sky beyond was placidly inviting.

Finally, Steve Lame Boy was saying: "All right. All right. Have it your way, you fellows. We'll ask the girl to stand up. But first we should make the boy say whether he's guilty or not. That's the way it goes in a court. You fellows are so dumb in the head you don't know such things. It don't make no difference to me."

The listeners were amused by the outcome of the quarrel. They liked to see Steve taken down, since he had been putting on too many airs in his job as chief judge. They gave him the job just a year ago, and already he was getting too good for his own family. "Steve bought a pair of specs at the ten-cent store so he can read the law books." "Him! He don't know the hind side from the front of a book. He uses a book in the backhouse, that's all." He ignored the crowd and stuck to business.

"You, Pauline Delorme. Stand up. Is that your name, Pauline Delorme?"

Everybody saw then what a piece of filled-out, aggravating female flesh she was. Less than sixteen but ready for plucking. Men's heads lifted on their necks, their women stared, unsmiling.

"You know my name. You don't have to ask." She sulked, eyes down, flaming.

It was another score against Steve, the judge.

"This is a court, now. And you answer my questions. You tell us now if it's true."

The room turned silent quickly. Steve was coming to the meat of the matter at last.

"If what's true?"

"Why, what your father says, *fou!* Did this boy do something to you?"

Her breath caught so heavily that everyone heard it. It was like the sigh a woman makes. Men turned cold and hot. Steve should not be so hard on her, so suddenly.

"Did he do what?" Stubborn. Spiteful wench.

The crowd felt let down. Why did the slut put them off, when she knew what was what.

"Did he do it against your will?"

She sulked, said nothing.

Steve, looking lost, turned partially to his fellow judges. Let them ask something. But they ignored his eyes, looked the other way.

"You have to answer me now. This is a court and you have to answer."

"Oh, I do! How can a girl talk about herself with all these people here?"

Henry Twist saved Steve from further embarrassment. "See, here, now. I am the policeman. You answer the questions or you go to jail until you do."

"Well . . ." Steve coughed and looked away from his brother-in-law. "How many times? When was it, I mean. Tell us when it was, the first time, I mean."

"I don't know."

"Was it last winter or last spring or when?"

"It's none of your business!" Her head shot up stubbornly, her face scowling. She was not pretty, only rounded, filled out, thick limbed, warm breathed. And in her heart she was mean, too mean and stubborn to play the innocent for very long.

Dieudonné, without looking at her, saw that she was ugly. At heart, really ugly.

Steve had to pound on his desk before he could subdue the laughter. The girl had fire.

"Everybody shut up! And you, Pauline, answer, or I'll throw this case out of here." That was directed at the brother-in-law, to show him that he could take care of these things himself.

Sam Delorme, the man of dough, heaved at his daughter.

"I *dit te!* I'll take my whip to you! Tell what he asks, now!"

"Well, was it more than once?"

"Yes, it was. He caught me in the brush, two–three times. I had to do it. The pig!"

"Well, you were in the brush! What were you doing in the brush? Why did you go there so many times?"

A woman just back of Dieudonné whispered: "*Ça!* You old stupid! Why did she go to the brush indeed!"

Pauline sulked again. She would not answer.

Steve turned to his associates. "Why don't you fellows ask something now? You see how she is. I say we ought to throw this case out."

Cyril Blodgett, sitting at Steve's right, stood by the law. "You can't throw out a rape case, Steve. That's serious business. Now you got to have the girl tell you the place exactly, and the date. You always got to know the spot where a crime was committed. Marks the spot."

Down the room a voice guffawed. "We all know the spot this time, Cyril! Ask her something hard." Laughter came up in a rush of wind which the judges, wisely, did not try to stem.

Steve waited until dignity won over confusion, then he resumed. "You, Pauline Delorme, tell us now when this happened."

She stamped her audacious high heels. "In March, then."

"Oh, in March, then. Before the snow was gone?"

"He made me go to the hayshed."

"The hayshed on your father's ranch?"

"Yes."

"He made you walk to the hayshed every time?"

Her temper broke there. She stamped and shrieked and fell wailing into her chair.

"Well, old stupid! You don't have to be like a bear," the woman back of Dieudonné shouted.

It was some time before the room became quiet again. Then Cyril Blodgett began to advise Steve once more.

"She's no good now. Better call the boy. Find out if he admits it."

Steve shook his head in grudging agreement.

"Dieudonné Leroux. Stand up!"

The boy, red-faced once more, straightened his shoulders as he stood up. He glared at the fumbling judges. Their combined idiocy made him, who had already traveled in the world, feel pained.

"Did you do something to this girl last March?"

"Do what?" He snapped the question out.

Steve fumbled, got angry. "What she says. You know what I mean. Did you carry her to the hayshed?"

For the first time he turned to the girl, his lips parting mockingly. She was hunched forward, weeping to relieve her petulance.

"I never had to carry her anywhere. Paying for it was enough, without handling her around."

At that the court was thrown into an uproar. Fat Sam Delorme was waving his arms. "*Tu, chien! Sacré. . . .*" He wanted to murder the boy.

"Just as I said! *Comme je dit! Comme je dit!*" The women cackled, tongues dipping.

Pauline cried out in rage. "Shut your dirty mouth! My brother will black your eye. Just wait till he comes home!"

And in the midst of the noise and confusion, Dieudonné stood smiling and dreaming.

Something out of the four hundred years echoed in his skull. Men singing, perhaps. The room of ruins sluiced between the rock ways. Winds topping the spruce forest. The chanting and clamoring of a world coming to life in the hands of its workers. It was in Dieudonné's head, in his eyes. He saw it in the composition of tree tops and fleckless June sky in the frame of the window. It was that that made him look so calm. He waited.

Steve Lame Boy was gradually making himself heard. "I just want to ask this girl . . . I just want to ask this girl. . . . How old are you?"

"Sixteen, if it's any of your business!"

"You! I ought to throw you out! Instead, I'm helping you. Because if you was only sixteen you couldn't consent anyhow. That's rape. You, Dieudonné Leroux, do you understand that? It's rape just the same. Stop looking through the window and listen! I say it's rape just the same."

The woman in back of Dieudonné started a commotion. She was getting to her feet. She wore a hat like an inverted pot that came down over the upper part of her face. A corset strapped tightly to the billowing figure pressed her breath out in gasps.

"You, Steve Lame Boy, you got to listen to me!"

"Watch your tongue, Mrs. Belvoir. This is a courtroom and you got to wait till you're asked."

"You listen to me! You don't know so much! If that little snip don't know how to consent then I never saw one that did."

Fat Sam Delorme bellowed and heaved himself at the inverted pot. A chair got in his way, luckily, and he made a muddle of three spectators. He got no nearer. Pauline screeched. Dieudonné smiled more mockingly.

Mrs. Belvoir shouted above the commotion and made herself heard.

"I ought to know about her, I guess, and the whole family. You, Fat Sam, just shut up and let me tell the truth once. This boy wasn't the first one, neither. What else could you expect with no mother in the family and these three girls growing up like weeds and Sam too fat to see beyond his belly. I was his housekeeper until I quit and so I ought to know. As for that Pauline, there was always somebody waiting down there in that brush. I tried to stop it, but what could I do? I could hear the boys calling "Are you coming?" and first thing I knew she would be smoothing that bushy head of hers and wandering off down there. I tried to whip her once and she hit me. Wonder I wasn't poisoned."

Henry Twist, chief of police, with urging, was asserting his authority on Mrs. Belvoir. But he could not stop her last shot.

"You fools, men! I said what I had to say, and now maybe you'll have some sense about that boy. That girl can't consent! My eye!" She sat down so forcefully that the inverted pot bobbed over one eye. She won applause from all the women.

Disregarding the turmoil as best as he could, the judge leaned forward to ask the girl. "Can you swear that you did not give your consent?"

Pauline screeched, "Sure I can swear it! I never consented to nothing with that cheapskate!"

Henry Twist confused the matter and made Steve's face turn sour by remarking, "A person can't swear to anything that's under age, can he, Steve?"

"I'm gonna throw this case out in a minute. Who's judge here, I want to know!" Steve turned his sour gaze on the crowd, and finally singled out the girl's father.

"What do you mean letting your girls grow up this way? It's your job to look after them, not this court. Why don't you see to them, then they wouldn't be dragged in here. Is your girl going to have a baby?"

Fat Sam stared stupidly for a moment. It did not sink through his corpulence at once that he was being scolded. When he did get the sense of it his wrath began to beat. His feelings were wounded. He rose up with the awkward labor of an infant and cut loose on his daughter, exploding French-Cree epithets in her ears.

"Just see now how you have them laughing at papa! Why don't you behave! How am I to see after you every minute? And why didn't you tell me you are going to have a baby? Little *stupide*! Well, what now. Are you having a kid, or not?"

Pauline shrugged impatiently, "Of course, I am having a kid! What's so new about that!"

"Ay–yay–yay!" Sam rocked his head in his hands and turned upon Steve.

"Somebody's got to marry her! That's up to you now. What's the good of sending this boy to the reformed school if the girl's that way? You got to make him marry her. I can't take care of another one."

Steve nodded in scant sympathy. "Let's just ask the girl . . . let's ask her. . . . You, Pauline, stand up. Do you want to marry this boy?"

The girl tossed her head in Dieudonné's direction in time to catch his [working] look. She made a face at him, darting out her tongue.

"Him? Not on your life! Put him in the jug. He did it to me and he's got it coming."

"There, you see," Steve gestured to fat Sam. "Your girl won't marry him. As for him doing that to her . . . I ain't convinced he did. I'm going to throw this case out of here. What do you fellows say? Shall we throw it out?"

Mrs. Belvoir bobbed up once more, the inverted pot pushed back from her brow. "Are you getting some sense at last, you fool men? Of course, she won't marry him! And it would be better for the boy to go to jail than marry her kind. You got to turn that boy loose. You'll have it on your souls until Judgment's Day if you don't."

"Mrs. Belvoir!" Steve's bellowing voice, after several failures, broke into her harangue. "You ain't the court. You ain't a witness even. We'll settle this matter right. I'm going to just talk to this boy. . . . I'm going. . . ."

The boy was gone!

Commotion. Laughter near the entrance where the crowd seemed to have lost interest in the front of the room and was pushing and scrambling to get outdoors.

Horse galloping away.

Shouts. "He's beat it! Hurrah for Doney!"

Steve Lame Boy arguing with Henry Twist, the policeman.

"You got to get him back. It's your job. So after him!"

"Hell! You was going to turn him loose. What's the use?"

"But that's the law! He's run away from the law, and you got to bring him back."

"An . . ." Henry made an obscure sound.

▽

Galloping down the street Dieudonné heard news which stopped him short.

"Le Premier is dying! I've come to tell everybody."

Now that was such incredible news that Dieudonné felt a complete shift of interest. The contents of his [. . .] mind emptied itself and an entirely new set of thoughts and feelings rushed in. It was as dramatic as walking from sunlight into midnight blackness. Le Premier, dying, was one of the things that would never happen. It had not been ordained. Le Premier had been a pillar of the world, one of the four corner parts that held up the sky. He could not crumble away.

Quite forgetting that people were rushing out of the schoolhouse in search of him, he held his horse still and listened to what Tom Shortman, the newsbearer, was saying.

"The priest is coming already. The doc's there now. They say he's singing in his bed."

Tom, who was Dieudonné's distant cousin, was pulling his horse's bridle once more, ready to dash away.

"Le Premier's dying!" he shouted to someone approaching down the street.

Le Premier, his uncle of the snow-white head, dying!

At any rate, it decided his next move. Dashing out of the schoolhouse, where that stupid trial had labored, he had wondered which way to run for it. He had to get out, of course. Not that he minded. It was time. Only he hated to be driven out.

But all this was swept out of mind. Le Premier, dying, was four hundred years gasping its end. There would be no continuity after him. It was because of Le Premier, indeed, that Dieudonné had some sense, slight as it was, of the four hundred years.

En roulant ma boule, roulant . . .

That was Le Premier.

Basques and Bretons on the cod banks, Normans coming ashore up the St. Lawrence; Poutrincourt, Pontgrave, Champlain—those old names; Radisson and Groseilliers; later Chevallier de Troyes, Pierre Le Moyne d'Iberville—all these lived in Le Premier's long tales and endless songs. Not the names, for Le Premier was no book [lover], but the story, rather the long song of ruin and dark and a world of silence come to life.

Le Premier carried the whole, pregnant sense of it in the [length] of his snow-white hair, in his windy laughter. With Le Premier dying, a world was dying. Dieudonné sensed it, wonderingly.

He turned his horse northward out of St. [Larin], touched his heels to the responsive flanks, and as he raced away from the last straggling buildings, a disturbed dog ran out in momentary pursuit.

"*Va t'en!*" He shouted back, bending close to the horse's neck.

On his right were the mountains, still snow-capped in June, their perfumed canyons [. . .] by shafts of sunlight piercing a blue mist. Riding in the open prairies, he looked toward the mountains and had a sense of the stillness which lived there. Stillness and peace and eternity . . . what Le Premier was approaching.

He was running too fast. There were ten miles to travel. He pulled the sorrel horse down to a trot, after noticing that he had begun to darken with sweat.

He began to overtake people traveling the same road . . . whole families in wagons or buggies, with other couples riding horseback or walking. And as he rode past, they shouted . . . "Tell *le vieux* we're coming! Tell him to wait for us!"

That spurred him on again. The thought of Le Premier trapped in bed and waiting for a spasm to carry him off reminded him that the old man had been asking to see him for weeks past and Dieudonné with a young man's acceptance of immortality had not gone. He raced on, as if he could make up by hurrying for his long delay.

June dust rose lazily, a sweeter dust than would rise in midsummer heat.

Dieudonné had been a favorite with the white-bearded half-giant. Perhaps that accounted for the strong attachment the boy felt for him. Out of God only knew how many children and grand-children, Dieudonné, last-born of Le Premier's infant sister, had always been the old man's pet, the one who was given knee rides, who drank from the old man's cup, whether it contained coffee or whiskey, and who had learned to love the booming of the old man's voice in the spinning of a story.

The boy's mind was hazy as to the details of Le Premier's life, of the significance of his living. As Dieudonné put it together, the snowy hero was a kind of Adam, a kind of first man on the earth. In an earlier year, it would have been impossible to conceive of the old fellow as having had father and mother, as having once been a heavy-headed baby sucking up mother's milk. Even to think so would have disgusted the boy. Now he knew he should know better, since he was turning man, but he still preferred not to contemplate such unheroic thoughts.

He did know that Le Premier had come down from the fur trade, from Red River, from Fort des Prairies, the riverways of the North, *le pays d'en haut*. He knew this because it was in every word the old man spoke, every song he sang. And to those men of the North, there had been no world before they came along and set the bounds to it, and there had been no men worthy of the name until they set the pattern. And of course, Red River was the mother of them all. Red River of the North—*la rivière rouge. Ave Maria.*

He had the vivid imagery of a song which went back and back into mistiness, like a living thread of water which you might watch from a grassy hilltop inlaying its silvered course in the prairie and disappearing with a final gleam on the horizon's uncertain edge. So it was a song, *En roulant ma boule, roulant,* rather than a connected narrative, which he knew so intimately. Yet it was a song which gave him a full sense of the narrative. Words would never fill out any more vividly the passages which he knew by knowing images alone. *En roulant ma boule, roulant* was four hundred years of history captured in a phrase as no book would ever catch it, and Dieudonné was but a stripling with all of life before him in which to give verbiage to sensory gropings.

Le Premier stood as a terminal to that phrase. Dieudonné knew that, but he had never known that some day the phrase would close forever. That was where he was still a child, still enamored of his hero. And that was why, now, he clamped his unspurred heels hard against the sorrel horse's flanks. He should have been visiting the old man continually in recent weeks, and instead he had been running rather wildly with a pack of boys who did not interest him in the least, except as an outlet for the exuberance which grew naturally out of his system. He was remorseful, and a little frightened.

Le Premier, dying. The song undoing.

Meat for God

▷ ▷ ▷ The old man, the old buffalo hunter, had come to this. He would be dozing on his doorstep and, dreaming, would rise up to take his gun from the wooden rack just within reach of the door, and then his daughter would rattle a pot.

"Papa! Wake up! You and your old gun!" It had happened not once but frequently. It had come to that.

There he sat, Sam Peël, the spring sun in his eyes, lighting no answering fire. There he sat on the doorstep. He could have been taken for an Indian. His white hair hung in two thin braids over his chest, the ends wrapped in fur; on his head a flat hat with broad brim, aged to smoke yellow, with leather thong passing under his chin and loose ends hanging. He was clothed in old blue serge, the coat buttonless and the trousers kept up by a beaded belt with leather ties instead of a buckle, and moccasins on his feet. But he was no Indian; brown and wrinkled as was his face, Sam Peël was all French—he had been a long time forgetting it.

Sitting that spring morning on a log hewn half through, which was his doorstep, he had to remember that a gun was no good to him. If he fired it the game warden, no doubt, would come and take it away. "You shoot your gun? All right. You go to jail." That was how they talked now to a man who had come before any of them—fence-

diggers, land-plowers and house-builders—none of them understood
by whose leave they had taken possession.

"Gran'père! Old man! I'm goin' huntin' bear. You can come and
skin 'em."

That was Le P'tit, round faced, serious. He was making for the
woods with the bow and arrows which Sam Peël had fashioned for
him out of red cedar. The old man would have gone along but he had
a stiff leg that morning. He remembered that going to the woods with
the nine-year-old was no light labor. He would be told that he
dragged his feet, that he couldn't keep up, that he couldn't see anything, that he couldn't crawl on his belly the way you had to do when
you were looking the enemy over. A nine-year-old knew the rules.

From Sam Peël's cabin the land sloped down. He could sit in his
doorway and have the whole thing before his eyes. Westward was the
pass, an undulation in an unbroken line of blue-green mountain;
there he had come slopping through the rotten snow of winter's end.
Lost, starving, fevered—he remembered it easily. At the end he had
been quite out of his head. He had thrown his gun away; his axe went;
his pack of remnants—a scrap of dried meat, a handful of flour—that
had been dropped as he wallowed in snow down the mountainside (it
was sixty years ago; but sitting in his doorway and looking at the very
notch in the mountains through which he had crawled he had every
sensation of it); and presently when he saw an Indian standing before
him he dropped on his knees and waited for the thrust of steel in his
back. His mind held no pictures of the stout arm which had raised
him from the snow.

Sam Peël was an old man now, and what his eyes saw was more
than the land sloping downward and a town built where had been an
opening in the forest. His cabin was above, and out of it, and yet he
belonged to the town; he dared not turn his back upon it, and at any
rate there was nothing to turn to. The openings in the forest were all
crosslaid with streets, and houses piped smoke upward to overlay the
sky. This was his waiting place.

Had it not been for Susette and Le P'tit it would not have been
bad, waiting. Had he none but his own old bones to finger under the
pinched skin, he could have taken it sagely. But it was otherwise.
Susette, just now, was making a clatter with an empty pot. She was

singing that gay song: *Les pommes de la Ronde Prairie Croissent si grand.* . . . One's mouth watered at the words. Le P'tit, he whose eyes were so sharp and his expression so serious, was off in the woods somewhere—"huntin' bear."

The old man could chuckle at that, but after a moment the insistent worry was in his eyes. Life was not easy now. You could not go to the woods or out on the prairie and get it. Le P'tit could be allowed to go about boasting of catching bears; there was nothing, scarcely a mild bird or flag-tailed squirrel, which he need fear. And there was a game warden. A man with a badge who rode about and told you when you could shoot your gun.

There were few who knew of Sam Peël. When he walked in the streets of St. Xavier, taking a slow step over a loose joint in the plank sidewalk, he was just an old man. His soundless tread attracted no attention. There was nothing in his slight build and stooped shoulders, or in his mild way of speaking, to suggest that he had laid the trail which others had been happy to follow. The few who did know him had not profited by the new day. They had as little as he—a sad horse or two, a wagon with no two wheels leaning at the same angle, and at home an empty pot. When he rested at their cabins they made him a meal of his own kind, of slaughter house refuse.

In his doorway, he could look out and see the whole of it. The land sloped down to the houses of St. Xavier: the sun flashed teasingly in his eyes from the windows down there. His own cabin was window-less—just a hole in the wall over which a blanket was hung in cold weather. There were a hundred buildings down there where, fifty years ago, lost and starving, he had been lifted from the watery snow and carried to shelter.

It was in an Indian tepee, the first he had ever seen from the inside, that he had opened his eyes at last. An older hand would have laughed at his fears, but to him that morning of awakening (he recalled vividly) was a moment of terror. Feeling himself sound of limb, he could but conclude that he was being fattened for the pot and turned his face to the tepee wall. Imbecile youth!

Old and calm as he was, he could never forgive that stupidity. The man who found him (dead long ago), took him as his brother; and it was through Sam Peël and the friendship which the Indians had for him that the Jesuits were invited to come and build their Mission; and after the Jesuits came a trading post; and then came an Army Fort; and then came the railroad; and then came laid-out streets and the fenced-up prairie: all of it was out of Sam Peël.

He could see it all as he sat in his doorway and looked down upon the crowded houses of St. Xavier.

Inside, Susette rattled an empty pot and sang of the *pommes de la Ronde Prairie*. But for them, for Susette and Le P'tit he would not have minded. An old man can live on his pipe, and for his pipe he could gather *kinnikinnick* in the woods. Nobody as yet had gathered it all or put a fence around it.

Susette was his youngest, and the only child of whom he knew the whereabouts. His old woman was sod by now. She had been the daughter of Big Ignace, the man who had stood above him that day in the wet snow and had not given him the taste of steel which his back had expected. He had just stood there, astonished by Sam Peël's want of spirit; and then had gathered him up like a sleepy child and taken him to his tepee. Sam Peël was no coward, as he proved later when he fought side by side with Big Ignace against those unrelenting enemies, the Blackfeet; perhaps it was the fever of starvation and fear (he had been lost for a week) which had unnerved him. His life had been determined that day.

Until then he had been Jean Pierre Marie Le Moyne, a name to evoke memories in Montreal and Trois Rivères, and beyond. He had gone out with the fur brigade, his first, and he never made the return voyage out to Fort William and across the Great Lakes and down the St. Lawrence. For all his waiting family knew, the wilderness had his bones. He had stayed where he had been found; those particular mountains and the particular patch of sky above them became dearer than anything he had left behind.

In time he forgot that he had ever been Jean Pierre Marie and was satisfied with Sam Peël, which was the nearest the Salish people, with no "r" sound in their tongue, could come to rendering his name.

Big Ignace's daughter—Florette was the name Sam Peël gave her—had been a good wife. He was proud of the skilful work she put into the buckskin clothes he wore (no man had better); and whatever the hour of day or night he might come home, he had never been kept waiting for food. In all their thirty years together he had never whipped her and she had never scolded. It was well that they were content with each other, because they never had any happiness in their children. The old life was going to pieces as their children were growing up and it was impossible to keep them in a tepee. One boy was shot because he looked like somebody who happened to be a horse thief; another was decapitated as he lay sleeping on a railroad track, evidently drunk; still another, put in the county jail for his part in a little fight, broke his neck when his foot slipped on the window sill as he was escaping; and so it went. Some were in prison now, others had gone off and had lost themselves. Sam Peël knew nothing of them, and it was just as well.

Susette, his last child, had come to live with him a year ago, bringing Le P'tit with her, and it was these two who made him realize that the old ways were completely gone. Somehow he had lived until now, alone for a long time, but he could not understand how he had managed it. He would be sitting there in the doorway and suddenly feel hungry. Without second thought he would go for his gun, resting on pegs behind his plank door, and then his head would clear. He had not shot that gun for ten years, except on New Year's morning. What should he shoot at? The housetops of St. Xavier? The stumps of his poor brush farm? There was a game warden now. He went riding around. "What's this meat you have? A steer? Show me the hide!"

"Papa! Put the gun back! You go to sleep there, then you jump up and go for your old gun. Just sit down, Papa."

It had come to that. A man who had hunted buffalo and had fought pitched battles, had to be told to put his gun down. He might shoot something!

Susette had been fat when she came to him with Le P'tit a year ago: "My man won't work. He drinks and lays around. And they throw him out of the poolhall. And now he's gone for good. They say he went to Spokane with a woman. She'll get her belly full. So now I have to stay with you, me and Le P'tit." She had been fat when she came saying that, but now she looked pinched in the face. Her bones came out of hiding.

An old man, past eighty (he had really forgotten how old he was), could not take his axe and split wood to sell down there in St. Xavier.

He had no horses—the last one had been killed for meat just after
Susette came—else he might go to the county and get a job driving
one of the green school wagons. It was difficult to understand how
everything had happened. Couldn't he have had all that land down
there in St. Xavier which they were selling now for five hundred
dollars a lot? Couldn't he go down there and tell them to get off, he
had come first?

The spring sun was not warm, but not cold either. An old man's
weathered skin hardly felt it. An old man's eyes thought nothing of
all this change: this snow seeping into the rocky hillside earth, these
waxen sprouts pushing up with caps of mud. An old man's head
worked at a puzzle.

If it was true that he might have had all that land down there, why
was it that he had to kill his last horse when Susette came to live with
him? Why was it that Susette had to go down to the slaughter
house? . . .

There was a sound in the nearby brush, there were running steps,
light steps, a shrill voice shattered the puzzle.

"Gran'père! Gran'père! Quick! The gun!"

Le P'tit, the serious, had stopped ten paces off and had already set
himself to return in the direction he had come. He was like the
second runner in a relay race, reaching for the baton, his feet beginning to carry him away.

"Quick, I say! Gran'père, can'tcha wake up!" The little fellow's
high excitement was giving place to sharp distress. His round face was
working as if in a moment he would cry.

Sam Peël was only now aware of the interruption. "Yes, yes, mon
petit. No doubt you have caught a bear, a very large one!"

"No! No! It's a buck deer! Just there!" By now the boy was wild
with impatience. He jumped about. Would the old man never get to
his feet? Would he never get his gun? Could he not understand that
he had just seen that big fellow push his high head through a thicket
of young spruce and stand listening? He might be gone even now,
though Le P'tit had crept along the ground like a dog, leaving his bow
and arrows behind, and had come as fast as he could run. He was
there, not a hundred yards off. Perhaps he had come down from the
mountain for green grass. Old man! Get a move on!

"A deer, you say? Mon petit, it was a cow! There has not been a deer on this mountain since your mother was a babe—Very well. It is a deer and I am coming."

The little fellow had a way of bossing one around. When he played a game, he played it hard. Sam Peël, before now, had learned to give in. Here was another of his games. In his make-believe he had turned a cow, perhaps a heifer, into a deer. He might as well have made it a buffalo. He did not intend to load his old gun, but the boy, eying him sharply, reminded him of the oversight.

"Gran'père! Put a bullet in. We got to have fresh meat."

It made Sam Peël smile. He watched the boy turn into the brush, gesturing for caution. He would have made a good hunter, if there had been anything to hunt. It was a born gift. The old man was diverted from his troublesome round of thought. He had slipped a fat cartridge into the old Springfield rifle (there were precious few of those cartridges left, but then he had no use for them), and his step quickened to the boy's enthusiasm. Susette had seen him take the rifle down and he had to call back:

"The little one has something, over here in the woods. He says we'll have fresh meat. So get the pot ready."

Susette sniffed. "You two—you babes. If you could shoot a sack of potatoes, now, that would be something. Vas donc!"

What upset Sam Peël was his coming upon the deer's tracks. It staggered him, so that he began all at once to tremble and to perspire. He got down on his knees and looked closely. There was no mistaking the sharp hoof marks. He could have wept. He could have kissed the ground. Not once in these long years had he seen a sight so pleasant. It was beyond fancy. Such a big fellow, too! The tread was heavy.

"My dear one! My beauty! Why didn't you say it was not a joke! What a smart fellow you are!" He was chanting so loudly that Le P'tit had to hush him.

By that time the old man was ready for business. His trembling was over. A glance told him which way the deer was heading and what direction he would have to take to come upon him. He recalled, with dismay, that he had taken just one cartridge. What an old fool! But it would do. One shot was all he needed. He who had shot buffalo by the hundred. . . .

He had a moment of remembering other times like this. The excitement that seized everyone when news was brought that game had been found. Perhaps the whole camp had been sitting for weeks with nothing but boiled black moss to eat; the wind would be sweeping veils of frost and snow across the sky; hungry eyes would stare into tepee fires—and then a runner would arrive urging a spent horse. More hunters were needed. Horses were to be brought. At once the camp would be in an uproar. Children would begin to shout. Dogs would howl. The women would sharpen their knives. Fires would be kindled. Then the hunters would go dashing out of the camp. And afterwards there would be the night of forgetting how black the days had been. A bragging man would be heard to exclaim: "From now on, meat is my food. I eat no more of this *tripe de la roche*." An old woman would roll a piece of meat in her toothless mouth and murmur: "Peace, fool! It's such as you that brings this blight upon us. When you learn to eat what you have it will be easier for those who have to live with you."

Sam Peël's eyes were pleasantly afire. Now there was no slowness about him. He ordered Le P'tit to the rear. It was no time for child's play. The old man walked stealthily and with energy. The gun was in his right hand, balanced, ready. From time to time he paused to listen for the sound of crackling brush. The buck was in no hurry. He was down here scouting the land. That was evident from his spoor. One could see where he stopped and sniffed the wind. There was a smell of green grass on the air. That was what had the old buck stirred up.

When finally he heard the sound for which he had been listening, the rest followed in almost the same breath. Brush cracked. Sam Peël stopped dead. The rifle was in both hands, half-raised. The gesture was old and familiar. It was a moment of supreme confidence. He could hold his own, thus and smile mockingly.

The big buck, immensely tall at the shoulder, pushed through an undergrowth of frazzled brambles and stopped. His nose was in the air. Something was wrong. His front feet had jutted out together, braced. He snorted. Then he raised his front quarters, was pivoting, when Sam Peël's big gun exploded. The echo of it rolled up the mountain. He had been right. One cartridge was enough. The buck's front legs failed him. His hind legs lashed out convulsively and he shot forward, his chest plowing the earth. That was all.

The moment was complete. It was achievement in an old and beloved art. But it was brief. The old man's joy was suddenly gone. He did not move after he had fired. The gun was still half-raised. He was not looking at the fallen buck. The clamor his gun had made, the fearful, continuing echo of it, had struck him dumb with terror. The good God! Who might not have heard that shot! He had forgotten what a throaty blast the old piece gave off. The echo crashed and crashed in his head. It would never stop. He could not silence it. What if the game warden had heard it! What if he should come on the run! Sam Peël did not know whether it was the deer season or not. He did not understand those things.

Le P'tit had run forward to the kill, and like a happy dog going to retrieve, he danced about. "Gran'père! You shot him dead! He doesn't move! One shot, and he's dead!"

For a long time Sam Peël heard nothing. His lips were moving. Words were uttered: "Old fool! Now you've done it! Old fool! Now see!"

Then he heard Le P'tit, still shouting: "Shot him dead! Gran'père, that was the best shot in the world!"

What was that? The good God! The child was telling everybody! They would all come after him—the sheriff, the judge, the soldiers. He would have to hide himself. Or he could—

"Le P'tit! Say not a word to Susette but run quick to the house. Understand me, child! Not a word! There's pitch pine kindling under the stove. Bring it! Say it is for Gran'père and Susette will not stop you. Hear me? Not a word."

The boy questioned and was slow in starting, but at last he set off as fast as his legs would take him.

"Don't skin him, Gran'père! Wait till I come!"

Sam Peël worked fast. First his big gun, to which he had clung these years, believing it to be his oldest and best friend; he took it and laid it across the slaughtered buck. Then he rushed about. He grabbed up dead wood, branches of trees, windfalls, old brush. Armload after armload was heaped upon gun and deer. He worked without

pause. His ears strained at hearing. Was that a footfall? Was a horse-
man approaching? Faster! More wood!

Here was Le P'tit! Here was the pitch pine!

"Never mind, Le P'tit! Never mind! There will be roast venison for
the good God. Don't grudge it. Don't weep, mon brave. See how
quickly the fire goes! There, my dear, it has all caught. We'll go to
Susette. She was right. You can't shoot a sack of potatoes. We'll tell
her that."

That night there was no meat for supper. But that was nothing
new.

Snowfall

▷ ▷ ▷ The Indian sitting in the chair was old, but not so old that he wind-tottered. He was dry fiber, with stooped shoulders. His hair, colored like the ash of a burnt-out log, hung in side braids with the ends coiled neatly in red felt. His blue serge suit, buttonless and baggy, had traveled a long way from its lower Broadway fabricator. Slit eyes that twinkled, bland smile. This was Henry Jim.

He was saying something about selling a team of horses. Something as simple as that.

The Indian agent stirred out of his preoccupation. His smile, which broke slowly on his heavy face, had a quality of friendliness, a kind of enduring tolerance. He had been barely conscious of the Indian's approach, of his noiseless gliding toward the chair at the left of the desk. Now he pushed aside the papers on his desk top and waited for the Indian to speak again.

"My team, the big bay ones." The old man's voice was thin and wavering, but not unpleasant.

"The big—You mean your team?"

"Eh. The team."

"What then? Are they sick?"

"No. Not sick. I want to sell."

The spreading smile receded. The agent's gray eyes glinted to an opening uncertainty.

"It's a good team, Henry. You got lots of horses, ponies, cow horses. Good enough. Why don't you sell some of them? Save the team."

Henry waved it aside. "Everybody got that kind of horses. Nobody will pay money for that kind."

No denying that. The man behind the desk straightened out of his relaxed position and regarded the papers before him. A trifling frown gathered his eyebrows nearer. He was forced to express his real concern.

"Let's talk about this, Henry. Here on Two Buttes Reservation—" his gesturing hand swept toward a window view of rolling hills, scrub-timbered, well-grassed, and of a broad valley sweeping northward— "you're the best rancher we have. Most years white men have to buy hay from you. They say, 'Henry, how is it you got hay to sell when ours is gone?' They respect you for it. Isn't that so? Now you want to sell your team, a fine team. I helped you pick them out. How will you get your haying done? Cow ponies are no good for that."

Henry Jim ignored the question. "I want to pay my debts."

"Pay your debts?" It sounded more and more irrational, quite unlike Henry Jim. The government man's frown furrowed deeper. "Your debts are small. Nobody is looking for you to run off. It's August already. Almost fall. Pay your debts when you sell some hay. Or if you want to borrow a little cash—"

The suggestion was waved aside.

The old man was rising to his feet, a little shakily, but with the strength of a settled spirit. He wanted no further talk. He was distracted, remote. He had not come to the office to be humored. One was always missing those signals.

The warm August afternoon pressed in and made the room more stifling than it had been. Voices speaking beyond the office wall emphasized the silence that followed the broken thread of speech.

The agent rose with the old man, showing his uncertainty by getting his feet entangled in the spread legs of his swivel chair and almost falling. He got to the door just as Henry Jim stood ready to open it.

The Indian paused and turned part way round to face his agent. His dark eyes, looking rather watery, seemed not to focus but look at far things. Obviously he was addressing the agent, but only his words showed it. His thought was somewhere beyond.

"When the time comes, when snow flies, I will send for you. I will tell you then."

"Yes, Henry. Of course. Send for me and I will come any time."

It was a relief to have something to say. The Indian had moved through the door and out into the strong August sunlight before the agent could think of asking what the Indian meant. What was it he wanted to talk about that he couldn't mention now.

Ephraim Morse stood looking across the agency compound. An Indian superintendent had to be a busybody. That was the worst part of the job. If one of his wards came wanting to sell a team of horses to pay his debts, the superintendent was expected to look into it. "Now, now," he must say, "why do you want to do that? If you knew better, if you knew as much as I do, you wouldn't. Take my word for it."

Always the matter of seeing to it that the Indians knew what they were doing. And always, too, the sense of working against time, of time looking over your shoulder, nudging you. Someone would be waiting, not simply for a letter from Washington with instruction on procedure, but for a chance to live or to bury the dead. Always someone waiting. Time looking over your shoulder.

"We don't just grow old," Ephraim Morse would tell his wife, explaining himself and his brothers in service. "We pass through ten lifetimes. We become a walking tomb of people who died waiting for a short word from us, when we had to wait on somebody else. We bury them, then carry them with us." And his wife would nod an assent that was at once silent and remote.

$$\triangledown$$

The August days ran on, searing the leaves of the cottonwood trees to crispness. The reservation roads were piled deep in yellow dust, which every puff of hot wind tossed high against the horizon of mountains. Wheat harvesters rolled their heaped-up golden wagons across the stubble fields.

Then there was a morning in September—the twenty-second, Ephraim Morse noted when his secretary flipped over the page of his calendar pad—which began in sunshine, a sort of lukewarm sunshine, with a strengthening wind blowing out of the northwest. He left his office in mid-morning to inspect some repairs being made on the horse barn over at the edge of the compound. He noted then that the wind had piled windrows of clouds all across the sky. The sun had paled until even the spot it had occupied went quite gray. The wind turned colder.

He was down at the barn talking to his carpenter when Henry Jim's forty-year-old son, Aloysius, came across to meet him. The son was grave and halting, traits of countenance and manner that reminded one of the father. He did not call out or speak at once, just came up and halted.

"How is your father?" Morse asked, offering his hand.

The son, moccasin-footed, tipped his head upward until the straight-edge brim of his hat made a line with the topmost wave of the background mountains. He was squinting at the blowing clouds, looking for something which his eyes told him was not there.

"It is going to snow," he said in a flat voice that suggested utter lack of faith in his own words.

"Snow!" Morse exclaimed and looked to the sky in bewilderment. On the twenty-second of September? No. The wind would grow still stronger and blow the clouds away by noon. Or it would die down and there would be rain. A cold autumn rain. That was the best his weather sense could make of it.

"Maybe rain, Aloysius. But not snow."

Aloysius shifted his feet, looked from this to that, worried.

"My father said it would snow and asks you to come to see him."

Morse looked more sharply at Henry's son. He didn't know him well enough to judge his mood. Was it fear that showed in his eyes?

"Is he sick, then?"

Aloysius shrugged his heavy shoulders. The rawhide thong which passed from his hat and tied under his chin swayed its loose ends with the gesture.

"He sleeps a lot."

"Sleeps a lot?" Was that bad?

Aloysius did not expand on the statement.

"Tell me, Aloysius. What does your father want to talk about?"

To that there was no response, only a silent regard which Morse found baffling.

"And why does your father want to sell his horses? Will he quit farming?"

He might as well have saved his breath. Aloysius only shrugged.

Driving his bay-matched mares that September day, Morse wished he had stopped by his house to put on warmer clothing. The wind had a bite to it. It drew water to the eyes. If his wife knew he had gone off wearing only a summer coat—

As he neared the end of the five-mile drive and looked upward to where Henry Jim's ranch lay outspread on rising ground, he was forced to realize anew how well the old full-blood had caught the white man's idea. Not only were the fields fenced, but the barn and house lots were enclosed separately; there were gates in good repair and fastened shut. Machinery was sheltered. There was an order in it that went according to the book.

His smiling recognition was jarred suddenly. In the barn lot, looking toward the road on which he passed, was one of the mates of Henry Jim's team. He looked closely to verify his first impression. He was not mistaken. Only one horse was in sight. The animal stood with its head up, evidently searching the wind for scent of the lost mate.

The inner cabin was something different, another world entirely. One faltered, letting the eyes adjust themselves to the gloom, being uncertainly aware of people sitting in silence back against the walls.

Henry Jim lay fully clothed on top of the bed, and his eyes, slowly following the agent, seemed to be the only part of him still muscled. He looked tired. Morse sat down, trying to keep his weight off of the roundless, spread-legged chair beside the bed. It was some time before he spoke.

"When men get our age they need rest once in a while. That's what it is. Not sick, Henry. Just a rest."

It was an amiable thing to say, so Morse thought, but he could not tell whether Henry Jim found it so.

One never knew, of course, what effect one's words had. These old fellows had a kind of courtesy which would not permit them, even if they liked you, to tell you what they thought of you. They looked at you through eyes which never gave anything away.

Morse tried to explain in his own thoughts what it was that his senses prickled to there in the cabin and which marked it off from the world outside. It was not one man's past, not one race's, but mankind's, it seemed. That was the sense of it. Was it the gloomy cabin which made him think so? And those confusing, old-as-earth smells? It seemed to be, in a moment's summary, history before there was history. A fragment split off from Asia, cradle of humankind—didn't someone say so? Or was this nonsense?

He couldn't tell by looking at Henry Jim, whose staring eyes had come to rest on Morse's face.

"A few days in bed and you'll feel better. Men our age need rest." He tried to make the silence sit more easily.

And then Henry Jim spoke, with unexpected clarity.

"Now it is going to snow," he said. Just that.

Morse faltered, almost agreeing before his rational mind impeded him.

"Snow? In September, Jim?"

The old man ignored the question.

"I have to wait until it starts before I can talk to you."

The agent reared back, irritated, yet willing to be patient. He had learned that much in twenty years.

"I try to follow you, Henry. My thought tries to go along, and then it stops. What is it you want to talk about?"

It was a stupid question, but Henry did not reject it. He even smiled, and let it go at that.

In a kind of helpless gesture, Morse turned to the others to learn what they were thinking—to Aloysius, who had just come in; to Henry's old wife, toothless and sightless; to relatives of greater and lesser degree—all sitting motionless, eyes averted, merging in shadow. He would learn nothing from them.

"Snowfall won't be soon." He tried to stay casual.

"Yes. Quite soon." Henry turned his face away, as if withdrawing from the contest.

It was just at that point Morse got the intimation of finality which, until then, he had been missing. He was immediately apprehensive, and sat up straight in his chair. Now he really had to know what was going on.

"Henry, when your people see you sell horses and quit farming—what will they do? Quit?"

That, he realized, was the special interest which had carried him at a fast trot from the Agency. It was a vital point. Because, after months of preparing field reports and receiving experts out from Washington, he had won approval of a program of increased expenditure on farm equipment. An enlarged effort to make farmers out of Indians. And what now? If Henry Jim gave up, retired to a moody living in the past, would plows rot to rust all over the reservation? Was the old man renouncing the faith that was work horses and machinery and fenced-up acres?

The old Indian stirred at the question. With great effort, he rolled part way on his side and looked at Morse.

The heavy breathing began to sound like roaring wind in the deepening silence of the room. As his voice emerged, the roaring subsided.

"You think I will be here, maybe. You want me to work my horses. But I am only waiting for snowfall. Then—"

Morse's eyes opened wide. This was really alarming. There was meaning in Henry Jim's words which had to be taken into account. This talk about snow obscured the real matter.

"I have to understand, Henry, if you want me to help. I have to know. Why did you sell just one horse?"

Henry Jim turned his head away.

"I can't talk about that now. When the snow begins to fall, you come. I will explain."

The agent knew when to stop and when to smile. He knew when talking had become useless. He rose uncertainly.

Stepping through the low doorway, Morse looked skyward and saw heavy clouds, looking as if they had been compressed into a solid. The wind was slackening.

Glancing earthward again, he reasoned. It never snowed in September—well, the Agency record said it didn't.

Aloysius was waiting outside, hands in pockets.

"What do you think—" Morse's question ended vaguely.

The forty-year-old son turned and stared toward the creek-and-willow-bordered pasture. Horses were down there, cow ponies, their tails flying in the cold wind. Their heads were up, uncertainly, as if they too sensed an unseasonableness.

"When it snows, you come, eh? He wants to say something?"

"Say what?"

A shoulder shrug. What Morse should have expected. You could go so far, and then that shrug. In twenty years, from Sioux to Apache, and now among these mountain people, these root-diggers, the gesture had not changed.

How many times had he gone lanternless into the nebulous world of Indian pattern, grasping at the airy substance of mythical ideas, looking for himself among the shadows.

"They are not like us," he told his wife, Clarisse, that night, for what to her must have seemed like the thousandth time. "The earth is more real to them—much. They're barely separated from it—each generation is born back to it, while we get further away all the time. We lose touch with our beginning, our senses get thick-skinned. But they are everlastingly sensitive. We call them fatalists, but perhaps their fatalism is hidden knowledge."

In dawn chilliness Morse heard his wife exclaiming, childishly surprised—"Why, Ephraim! It's snowing! I can't believe it!"

Morse thrust his head out of the bedcovers. What had he to do with snow? What had he dreamt—

His wife was up, raising higher a half-raised window shade.

"See! It's just begun. There's hardly any on the ground. It melts as fast as it lights."

By the time she turned from the window, wondering whether her husband would plunge outward into the day, he was on his way.

The five-mile drive was a journey into a fabulous land. It snowed sparsely and drearily, the sky hanging low and dark and wet. Prophesy lay in just such witch's weather, not in sunshine and bird song. What was the world? Was one held in hand, used, wore on one's body? Was it the power one extracted from machinery, from electrical impulse, from the brawn of a horse's leg? Or was the real stuff a thing of no dimensions, immeasurable, from which all things were predicted, and did one have to be as uncomplicated as Henry Jim to feel the flow of the inward current?

Long before he reached the end of the drive, he knew what Henry Jim had been talking about. It was even possible, he thought, looking back, that he had understood even on that August afternoon, but had been too rational to admit it.

Henry Jim lay listless abed, fully clothed in the serge suit from lower Broadway, New York City.

There were the same hushed, bunched forms in the twilight cabin. Morse's entering caused no stir. He stepped cautiously toward the bedside, found the spraddle-legged chair on which he had rested uneasily the day before.

The old fellow's eyes were closed and Morse first thought that he was asleep. He remembered what Aloysius had said. "He sleeps a lot," and wondered how long he would have to wait. Then the eyelids fluttered and Morse caught a gleam of glazed eyeball. But no stir of lips. No effort even at acknowledgment.

He surrendered then to the silence. He dared not go out in the fresh air to wait because he wanted to be there when Henry finally came awake.

His shoulders went slack and he seemed literally to plunge into the silence, as if he had plunged into a pool of dark mountain water. Once beneath the surface, only the things within his own head moved, round and round, trying to fit odds and ends together. First he tried to sort out the odors—smoked buckskin, so pungent that it overpowered almost all other smells, except strong pipe smoke. And he was sure that somewhere in the depths of the interior a pot of meat was boiling. These were only the known, the identifiable; and back of them was a hint of old earth itself, of mankind emerging from smoke-filled caves and battling the land and the beasts of the land, and arriving here in a shadowy cabin that was still part cave.

He wondered how it was that silence sat so easily with these people, while it produced such churning in him. He could not know. But he could guess that there was in them an overpowering sense of continuity, of things coming to them whole-made out of the past, against which their wills and their emotions never warred. While he, split from the past, felt the silence as a burden that strained muscle and nerve. He labored over each passing moment.

He was startled to find that Henry Jim had turned his head toward him and was watching him through weary eyes. Something like a smile pulled at his loose lips.

"The snow is here. Now I can tell you—"

Morse was wordless. For when the old man spoke, what was there to say, except perhaps to assert (which he did not think of doing) that he had seen faith work its way to its own inner core? It was surely faith—and yet, how did it work? What was the mechanism by which he knew?

There was still the suggestion of a smile when Henry spoke again. "I sold only one horse," he remarked, his voice gaining in strength. "I didn't need much money. A few debts. One horse was enough." There he hung for a moment, considering. "This now is what I have to say. This good horse I have left. I want to take him with me. It troubles me. I know things have changed. In the old days our relatives killed a horse and put it on our grave so we could travel beyond. Now it is different. I know that—"

He fumbled with one hand at his pillow, withdrawing from under-head a soiled bit of cotton, possibly a remnant of old shirt, which in his weakness he trembled at unrolling.

"This is left—"

A crumble of bank notes lay wadded in his hand, some loose ends protruding.

The agent received the offered wad, separated the individual notes, smoothed them on the bed's edge, leaning forward from his rickety perch. The money was old, limp, in different denominations, tens, fives, ones, over fifty dollars.

"You take this money. Put me in a white man's box. Bury me in the ground. Up there where my land looks over the river. You know the place, where the river cuts a high bank. Bury me there. And I want a looking-glass there. Turn it down river."

Again a silence held intact by the old man's gesturing spectral hand.

"It was my father stood on that hill and watched the first white men our people ever knew come up the river. It was his eyes first watched them. And since then we have all grown old watching the white men come. So I want this looking-glass to face down river and it will be my eye. I will watch what comes." A long pause, then: "You can decide about the horse. . . ."

That ended his talking. Henry Jim was tired. Mortal weariness. The twilight room perfected its mood of waiting, perhaps listening. The dust-powdered window light showed feebly that snow still fell.

Morse realized that he had to speak quickly, firmly, while old Henry was still within hearing. There was no time, this once, to await on instructions. So he spoke, and was startled to hear himself saying:

"We will do what you ask. Everything. You will have the horse—"

And then he thought, "My God! Will they all kill their horses after this?"

Henry Jim looked once more, fleetingly, then hooded his eyes under relaxing lids.

▽

When Morse went out, he saw the bay horse again. The animal stood at the fence, as before, and gazed with whited eye toward the cabin. Once, as the agent stepped near, the horse looked away and pawed at the snow-dampened earth, head lowered. Morse thought his nostrils dilated and quivered, as if the creature had whinnied. But there was no sound, unless it had been a sound beyond hearing.

He walked to the roadside fence and extended his hand. "Come, boy! Come, old fellow!"

The bay tossed its head impatiently and continued to gaze at the cabin. Morse felt his scalp prickle, not knowing what he had seen and felt.

Aloysius had followed Morse out into the open and now he came forward, with an air of hesitancy. He came to a full stop before speaking.

"I am glad," he said, in a tone of mild wondering, "you are doing this for the old man. None of us thought a government man would do it, and we were afraid when my father asked."

"That's all right, Aloysius. It wasn't much."

"It will mean a lot to him. He wanted that horse very bad. He didn't want a scrub horse."

"Sure, I know. He wanted his good horse." He had a sense of inward shuddering when he thought, in some other part of his mind, of what he was saying.

Then Morse asked, unable to hold back any longer: "How did your father know all this was going to happen—and why wouldn't he tell me before?"

Aloysius obviously had been waiting for the question, and he smiled.

"Oh, that. He was told in a dream. And he wasn't to speak of it until snow came. That was what the dream said."

"A dream? I see. I was afraid you were going to say that."

▽

So he turned to go home, feeling dejected. Twenty years had not done so much for him. It had led him to a world's edge and there deserted him, with no signposts forward. And all the time, in his office, were people waiting, blue forms, plans prepared by experts. A yearly report of progress was due.

He wasn't even sure what he would tell his wife.

Train Time

▷ ▷ ▷   On the depot platform everybody stood waiting, listening. The train had just whistled, somebody said. They stood listening and gazing eastward, where railroad tracks and creek emerged together from a tree-chocked canyon.

Twenty-five boys, five girls, Major Miles—all stood waiting and gazing eastward. Was it true that the train had whistled?

"That was no train!" a boy's voice explained.

"It was a steer bellowing."

"It was the train!"

Girls crowded backward against the station building, heads hanging, tears starting; boys pushed forward to the edge of the platform. An older boy with a voice already turning heavy stepped off the weather shredded boardwalk and stood wide-legged in the middle of the track. He was the doubter. He had heard no train.

Major Miles boomed. "You! What's your name? Get back, here! Want to get killed! All of you, stand back!"

The Major strode about, soldier-like, and waved commands. He was exasperated. He was tired. A man driving cattle through timber had it easy, he was thinking. An animal trainer had no idea of trouble. Let anyone try corralling twenty-thirty Indian kids, dragging them out of hiding places, getting them away from relatives and together in one place, then holding them, without tying them, until train time! Even now, at the last moment, when his worries were almost over, they were trying to get themselves killed!

Major Miles was a man of conscience. Whatever he did, he did earnestly. On this hot end-of-summer day he perspired and frowned and wore his soldier bearing. He removed his hat from his wet brow and thoughtfully passed his hand from the hair line backward. Words tumbled about in his mind. Somehow, he realized, he had to vivify the moment. These children were about to go out from the Reservation and get a new start. Life would change. They ought to realize it, somehow—

"Boys—and girls—" there were five girls he remembered. He had got them all lined up against the building, safely away from the edge of the platform. The air was stifling with end-of-summer heat. It was time to say something, never mind the heat. Yes, he would have to make the moment real. He stood soldier-like and thought that.

"Boys and girls—" The train whistled, dully, but unmistakably. Then it repeated more clearly. The rails came to life, something was running through them and making them sing.

Just then the Major's eye fell upon little Eneas and his sure voice faltered. He knew about little Eneas. Most of the boys and girls were mere names; he had seen them around the Agency with their parents or had caught sight of them scurrying behind tepees and barns when he visited their homes. But little Eneas he knew. With him before his eyes, he paused.

He remembered so clearly the winter day, six months ago, when he first saw Eneas. It was the boy's grandfather, Michel Lamartine, he had gone to see. Michel had contracted to cut wood for the Agency but had not started work. The Major had gone to discover why not.

It was the coldest day of the winter, late in February, and the cabin sheltered as it was among the pine and cottonwood of a creek bottom, was shot through by frosty drafts. There was wood all about them. Lamartine was a woodcutter besides, yet there was no wood in the house. The fire in the flat-topped cast-iron stove burned weakly. The reason was apparent. The Major had but to look at the bed where Lamartine lay, twisted and shrunken by rheumatism. Only his black eyes burned with life. He tried to wave a hand as the Major entered.

"You see how I am!" the gesture indicated. Then a nerve-strung voice faltered. "We have it bad here. My old woman, she's not much good."

Clearly she wasn't, not for wood-chopping. She sat close by the fire, trying with a good natured grin to lift her ponderous body from a low seated rocking chair. The Major had to motion her back to her ease. She breathed with asthmatic roar. Wood-chopping was not within her range. With only a squaw's hatchet to work with, she could scarcely have come within striking distance of a stick of wood. Two blows, if she had struck them, might have put a stop to her laboring heart.

"You see how it is," Lamartine's eyes flashed.

The Major saw clearly. Sitting there in the frosty cabin, he pondered their plight and wondered if he could get away without coming down with pneumonia. A stream of wind seemed to be hitting him in the back of the neck. Of course, there was nothing to do. One saw too many such situations. If one undertook to provide sustenance out of one's own pocket there would be no end to the demands. Government salaries were small, resources were limited. He could do no more than shake his head sadly, offer some vague hope, some small sympathy. He would have to get away at once.

Then a hand fumbled at the door; it opened. After a moment's struggle, little Eneas appeared, staggering under a full armload of pine limbs hacked into short lengths. The boy was no taller than an ax handle, his nose was running, and he had a croupy cough. He dropped the wood into the empty box near the old woman's chair, then straightened himself.

A soft chuckling came from the bed. Lamartine was full of pride. "A good boy, that. He keeps the old folks warm."

Something about the boy made the Major forget his determination to depart. Perhaps it was his wordlessness, his uncomplaining wordlessness. Or possibly it was his loyalty to the old people. Something drew his eyes to the boy and set him to thinking. Eneas was handing sticks of wood to the old woman and she was feeding them into the stove. When the fire box was full a good part of the boy's armload was gone. He would have to cut more, and more, to keep the old people warm.

The Major heard himself saying suddenly: "Sonny, show me your woodpile. Let's cut a lot of wood for the old folks."

It happened just like that, inexplicably. He went even farther. Not only did he cut enough wood to last through several days, but when he had finished he put the boy in the Agency car and drove him to town, five miles there and back. Against his own principles, he bought a week's store of groceries, and excused himself by telling the boy, as they drove homeward, "Your grandfather won't be able to get to town for a few days yet. Tell him to come see me when he gets well."

That was the beginning of the Major's interest in Eneas. He had decided that day that he would help the boy in any way possible, because he was a boy of quality. You would be shirking your duty if you failed to recognize and to help a boy of his sort. The only question was, how to help?

When he saw the boy again, some weeks later, his mind saw the problem clearly. "Eneas," he said, "I'm going to help you. I'll see that the old folks are taken care of, so you won't have to think about them. Maybe the old man won't have rheumatism next year, anyhow. If he does, I'll find a family where he and the old lady can move in and be looked after. Don't worry about them. Just think about yourself and what I'm going to do for you. Eneas, when it comes school time, I'm going to send you away. How do you like that?" The Major smiled at his own happy idea.

There was silence. No shy smiling, no look of gratitude, only silence. Probably he had not understood.

"You understand, Eneas? Your grandparents will be taken care of. You'll go away and learn things. You'll go on a train."

The boy looked here and there and scratched at the ground with his foot. "Why do I have to go away?"

"You don't have to, Eneas. Nobody will make you. I thought you'd like to. I thought—" The Major paused, confused.

"You won't make me go away, will you?" There was fear in the voice, tears threatening.

"Why, no Eneas. If you don't want to go. I thought—"

The Major dropped the subject. He didn't see the boy again through spring and summer, but he thought of him. In fact, he couldn't forget the picture he had of him that first day. He couldn't forget either that he wanted to help him. Whether the boy understood what was good for him or not, he meant to see to it that the right thing was done. And that was why, when he made up a quota of children to be sent to the school in Oregon, the name of Eneas Lamartine was included. The Major did not discuss it with him again but he set the wheels in motion. The boy would go with the others. In time to come, he would understand. Possibly he would be grateful.

Thirty children were included in the quota, and of them all Eneas was the only one the Major had actual knowledge of, the only one in whom he was personally interested. With each of them, it was true, he had had difficulties. None had wanted to go. They said they "liked it at home," or they were "afraid" to go away, or they would "get sick" in a strange country; and the parents were no help. They too were frightened and uneasy. It was a tiresome, hard kind of duty, but the Major knew what was required of him and never hesitated. The difference was, that in the cases of all these others, the problem was routine. He met it, and passed over it. But in the case of Eneas, he was bothered. He wanted to make clear what this moment of going away meant. It was a breaking away from fear and doubt and ignorance. Here began the new. Mark it, remember it.

His eyes lingered on Eneas. There he stood, drooping, his nose running as on that first day, his stockings coming down, his jacket in need of buttons. But under that shabbiness, the Major knew, was a real quality. There was a boy who, with the right help, would blossom and grow strong. It was important that he should not go away hurt and resentful.

The Major called back his straying thoughts and cleared his throat. The moment was important.

"Boys and girls—"

The train was pounding near. Already it had emerged from the canyon and momently the headlong flying locomotive loomed blacker and larger. A white plume flew upward—Whoo-oo, whoo-oo.

The Major realized in sudden remorse that he had waited too long. The vital moment had come, and he had paused, looked for words, and lost it. The roar of rolling steel was upon them.

Lifting his voice in desperate haste, his eyes fastened on Eneas, he bellowed: "Boys and girls—be good—."

That was all anyone heard.

▷ ▷ ▷ MONTANA

The Hawk Is Hungry

▷ ▷ ▷   My sister had come to spend the summer at my Montana ranch. It was a long ten years since I had seen her, I was fond of her, and I was hoping to keep her in the West. I wasn't subtle about it. I was bragging shamelessly about our advantages, I was ready to lie if need be.

My sister is an attractive person. She is young, she will always be young, she is pleasing to look at, and she enjoys herself. Her name is Anne Elizabeth, after a great-grandmother, whom she resembles, if the painting which hung in the library of our Connecticut home is to be trusted.

As I say, I wasn't being subtle in my campaign of persuasion. Every day I thought up something for the purpose.

"You laugh when you hear mention of the 'great open spaces,' but the fact remains, this is the place to live." I would make such a remark during our morning's ride—she likes horses and I had done everything to cultivate this interest.

"I know—splendid air—open-hearted people."

My fondness for Anne runs to such foolish lengths that she may take any sort of liberty with me—she always ends by regretting it and treating me with tender regard.

"Nonsense!" After one of her digs I tried to be stern. "We are really a free people out here. The American spirit is making its last stand here. Every man is his master. He believes in himself. We don't know anything about tenement life, ward politics, the factory system—all that. . . ."

Then she would smile, and I would know that she was ready to squash me once more. "Yes, you know so little about these things that you've let the Easterners get control of your power sites, your mines, and your politics. As for tenement life, look at your farmers. . . ."

"Ranchers, Anne!"

She gave me her broadest smile, in which, I suspected, was hidden a good bit of amused tolerance. We had reached home after the ride and we were hungry. We smelled our breakfast coffee as we came near the ranch house. If I have not already given myself away, I will make it clear that I am a bachelor, and that I keep a man and wife to cheer me up and to do the hard work. And after smelling the coffee, who could continue the argument? For once she did not wind up by calling me a romancer, a hopeless romancer, her pet term for me.

On that day I had promised to take Anne to visit the Brown sisters, Matilda and Beth. I had counted on the Browns to help me persuade Anne about the freedom of the West. They, like Anne, had been teaching school in one of those New York beehives; they had wearied of it, as her letters told me she had; and they had struck for freedom, coming here and taking up a homestead. They had talked to me about that. "We needed a change," they had said during one of our first conversations. "The city was stifling us and we needed a little free movement—needed to get our hands in the dirt." I had remembered their words. It wasn't any of my romancing. I had admired their courage. My coming to the West had been forced upon me by a physical and nervous system which had collapsed without much warning. The Browns had come by choice. That was what mattered.

Their homestead is high on a hillside. Some people have been unkind enough to speak of this as a piece of stupidity. "Who in hell would try to farm a hilltop, if he was in his right mind!" I've heard people say it. That wasn't fair. There wasn't much homestead land left when the girls came, and their choice was not the worst they might have made.

Their only water is a sluggish spring, and the soil up there is coarse and thirsty. In a dry summer—most of our summers are dry—they have the tedious task of carrying water to their garden. But what prejudiced people was the fact that the Browns had planted, and watered, a flower garden as well as the indispensable vegetable plot.

I told Anne about this and was surprised by my own vehemence in defending them against the harsh comments I had heard. These I put down to ignorance laughing at what it could not understand. High art in low company is nonsense. "You can see why they were misunderstood," I appealed to Anne.

I don't know what I had expected of her. A nod of the head, if it had been sympathetic, would have sufficed. All she said was, "You must take me to see them sometime."

That cooled me. I believe I changed the subject. At least I didn't tell her any more stories about the Browns, and there were more. There was one about the time Matilda washed the two pigs they had just bought, because "pigs are naturally clean" if given a chance, as their books on agricultural science informed them. And there was the time they were taken in by a rustic wag and on his advice had tried to buy "side-hill cattle," the kind with legs shorter on one side to make side-hill grazing more convenient. Without investigating these stories, I had dismissed them as fabrications; but the fact that I withheld them from Anne would indicate, I suppose, that I wasn't sure.

Still, I had introduced the subject of the visit and I wasn't permitted to let it drop. I suspect that Anne thought she might have some fun out of me. She had said, "I would like to see that flower garden built in defiance of the laws of nature, to say nothing of realistic neighbors."

Laughter and scepticism lay behind those words, and I shied. "All right, Anne. But I warn you, you may not enjoy them."

At that she did laugh. "I believe you're afraid to show them off!" I protested that I was nothing of the sort.

We drove the ten miles behind my fast bay team, setting out right after breakfast. On the way we talked about our childhood Connecticut, always a safe topic.

I am now coming to the part of this record which decidedly I do not like to recall. Our visit went so suddenly from a commonplace friendly call to—well, let's call it ridiculous and let it go at that.

The Brown place looked especially forlorn that morning. I had been there before, but I must admit that I had not noticed details. I suppose I was always full of thoughts about their independence of spirit and their making their own fate.

Their house was built of slab siding, refuse which most mills either burn or throw away, and the roof of a single slope was covered with tar-paper. Beside the house there was a shed for the chickens, which but for being smaller was equal to their own living quarters. The chicken house was shaded by a growth of wild elderberry bushes, around the roots of which the hens dusted themselves in holes worn by their bodies. There was a shed for the cow, a plain cow, no fantastic "side-hill" beast. Then there was a berry patch, with many dead bushes, the vegetable garden which gave them sustenance, and finally the flowers—against the walls of the house, in a round bed in the center of the yard, and a perfect nest of hollyhocks against the outhouse.

The eye took all this in in a single glance. I saw Anne look, and then look at me. I looked dead ahead. "This," she was saying silently (in my mind, of course), "you call superior to tenement conditions? It's true there is an abundance of fresh air! What a lot of fresh air!"

I had managed to get word to the sisters by calling their nearest neighbor on the telephone. So they were expecting us that Saturday morning. When they came out of the house a minute or two after we drew up, they had tidy aprons over their freshly ironed gingham dresses.

Anne slides very easily into any situation, and I should have known that there would be no difficulty in getting acquainted and settling ourselves. But I had become so apprehensive about Anne and the impression she would get of my prize exhibits that I did nothing but fidget.

"You've been here three years now, if I remember correctly," I observed at the first opportunity. I don't know what I expected them to say. I suppose Anne knew. I suppose it was written all over my face and in my manner, my eagerness to hear the Brown girls get rapturous over their manner of life. The words would not matter.

That was when things began to get ridiculous.

Matilda, the younger and the more quick-spoken, snapped me up.

"Three of the dreariest years mortals ever endured. If you called it half a century it wouldn't seem wrong."

Her voice was absolutely flat. For a moment we all only stared at her, Anne and I—more especially I—trying to get at her meaning. How seriously did she intend her words?

"Really," I said, trying to ignore that flatness in her voice, "it hasn't been that bad! Whenever I've seen you, you've both looked cheery—I would say happy. Always some new thing happening. . . ."

"Mr. Buck, you've seen very little of us—and you've never seen us after a broiling day when we've come in broken-backed from carrying water to our garden—you've never seen me get raving mad when that murderous chicken hawk carries off one of our precious few hens. . . ."

I was ready to drop the subject. It was the elder sister, Beth, who made the shift and got us back on safe ground.

I had noticed before that if at any time Matilda failed to make herself understood, or if one questioned her reasoning in a discussion, Beth came to her aid, perhaps not consciously. Matilda of course resented intrusions of that sort, and I had seen her contradict herself, apparently simply to embarrass her sister. Beth was mild and warm and devoted; Matilda was lean-faced, impetuous, argumentative, caustic, demanding.

"Everybody tells us we arrived in the driest years this country has ever seen. This hill, they tell us, used to be green all summer through. Maybe they're right. We only know what we've seen." She let it go at that and got Anne to talking about Connecticut, which was their homeland as well as ours. They came from Meriden, we from Hartford. Since they had been teaching in New York City not so many years before, it soon turned out that Anne and they had common acquaintances. After that, things went along pleasantly, almost gaily, for a while.

Matilda shook off the gloom which had resulted from our first exchange and was most eager in her questioning about life "back there."

"You've no idea what a treat it is to hear you talk," she said suddenly, her eyes shining.

The simple luncheon they served was made an occasion for bringing out their linen (they had a few pieces buried in a trunk) and silver, nice old-fashioned flatware. While the sisters worked at setting things in place and getting the food served up, Anne and I tossed words at them, never looking at each other. I saw her examine the surroundings in quick, shielded glances. I looked about too and felt depressed. The house inside lacked the shabbiness of the yard and garden, and it was scrubbed clean, but it was depressing.

The room in which we sat was hardly more than ten feet square and it was full of evidence of that rejected world (I could see now, realistically, that what had been left behind was more real, better understood, and better loved, than what they had come to)—an album of photographs, framed etchings and prints, a plaster cast of the Apollo Belvedere, Breton earthenware on a plate rail, and of course books, shelved against every vacant wall. I also saw a bookcase in the small room adjoining, the bedroom, and no doubt there were books stored away in boxes.

We looked at these things, Anne and I, and tried to make conversation. She avoided my eyes. She smiled gently when she caught the glances of the sisters. She was moved to tenderness. In fact, her reactions were what mine should have been, since I am supposed to be the more feeling person and she the more rational. And there I was, glum and depressed.

The table was set in the doorway, but it might as well have been on top of the stove. There was no shade outside but there even the noon sun was sufferable. As for that cabin, with its thin walls, low roof and small square windows, it was a perfect heat trap. We sat about the table and perspired, eating making it worse, and only slavish obedience to social custom kept us fully clothed and amiable.

Matilda took command of the conversation at the table. It seemed that we had all been in Brittany, at different times, and the talk turned first to the Quimper plates on the rack.

"We did get about," Matilda was saying. "Our two salaries combined meant an occasional summer in Europe, Christmas with our Connecticut folks, Easter in Bermuda. It wasn't bad, teaching."

I squirmed, not looking at Anne.

"There was that time we made an excursion in the Hautes Alpes. Motorbus trip. Remember, Beth? Like today, there were heat waves, layer on layer, and the peasants were on the mountainside above us, scything hay. We were in the last seat of the autobus, watching them. It was intolerable when we stopped, heat and dust, and burnt petrol. We wondered if the peasants did not hate us for carrying that smell into their mountains. Remember? We watched them, like brown moles on the mountainside, swinging their scythes. We said something like 'How patient and enduring. . . .' I often think of that when we're blistering on our hillside. Not very enduring, I'd say."

We laughed a little, without gaiety.

As we sat there I noticed a hen, a grouchy-looking bird of a dirty brown color, walk or rather stroll across the yard, obviously intent on looking us over. Coming near, she cocked her head at us and stood with one foot raised.

Beth saw me look. "That's Molly, the boss of the hencoop. She heard strange voices and has come round to investigate. None of the others, not even Tom the rooster, would stir about in this heat."

When Beth tossed out a crumb, Molly the hen showed some of her quality. If she had run excitedly for the tidbit, she would have attracted attention in the hencoop. Instead, she walked quietly toward the crumb, looked back once to make sure she was unobserved, then deftly clipped it with her beak and turned once more toward the humankind.

We all commented.

"A creature of sense."

"You could call it insight."

"Oh, Molly," Beth exclaimed. "She never makes a false move!"

It was left for Matilda to make the wry comment. "You see what we have come to. The neighbors think us fantastic, so they avoid us. Result, we're reduced to making conversations with the barnyard folk. You should hear us carry on. Some days you'd think we were a family of ten, the way we call out names. 'Tom, get out of the garden this minute! Susiebell—that's the guinea-hen—stop that racket!' "

Beth looked a little stung. "But they are like people! We've known people just like Molly. Bossy, fussy, always wanting her way, and getting it. Even Tom the old rooster has a way of giving in. The young rooster positively avoids her. He has his younger set. But that Molly— she'll even fight off the chicken hawk! The others, with old Tom in the lead, the silly thing, run at the first sight of his shadow."

That left us wondering what to say next. A kind of embarrassment had come upon me and I supposed that Anne shared it. I felt that under the surface of this neighborly visit were many quirky currents of meaning, hidden eddies of the subject which somehow one must avoid, deep pools of resentment and frustration. I began to wish we could be on our way—and we hadn't yet reached the dessert course.

Now it was Touraine, the château at Loches, and the little blue room with fleur-de-lys on the walls where Anne of Brittany had sat looking out upon the Loire flowing toward the sea—as the guide told it.

"At Chenancoux we stood in the room of that Medici woman. It was so different from Anne's little blue room . . . ," Matilda chanted, remembering more of her guidebook. "When we got bored by French chatter, we had tea at Thomas Cook's, upstairs. The English make those snug upstairs tea shops all over France."

If we could have kept to France and Bermuda and teaching in New York, all would have been well, and at the proper moment Anne and I would have started for home. Instead, we were swept suddenly into the full current of their hidden, complex lives.

It began when a shadow drifted across the yard. But before that, the rooster, with some of his hens in tow, had wandered out to share whatever entertainment Molly had found. They were together in a group, midway across the parched yard. Their beaks hung open. It was wretchedly hot just then. The sun blast withered every living thing, blinding animal eyes and giving a droop to green leaves. The utter quiet of the willows at the spring showed how breathless was the air. The faint piping whistle of a threshing machine in the valley announced the end of the noon rest. There was work to do. We at the table were wilted.

Molly the hen suddenly jerked her head erect. She looked toward the cabin, then off to the spring. Then a quick step of alarm. A moment later all the chickens had caught her awareness. Heads poked high. The rooster gave a throaty warning.

From my position at the table I had the best view of the yard and had seen that first stir of alarm. Matilda must have seen it almost as soon as I, for she reacted before the others. Her breath caught on a half-uttered sound.

The shadow streaked across the yard, was lost, then drifted back again from a different angle. It came to a pause. The hawk was directly overhead, descending.

Matilda reared up, on the point of screaming, but no sound coming. Her face, when I glanced up, was intense with pain. It chilled me.

The outcry of the chickens was shrill and wild. Wings fluttered, feathered bodies hurtled through the air, stirring small whirls of dust. The noontime stillness was suddenly loud with terror.

Molly gave ground slowly, backing away, wings spread and head lowered, scolding loudly. And then the bolt of death struck her, sprawling in the dust. A shower of feathers and scattering pebbles marked her last fight. Great wings flapped again. The sky raider was struggling upward. The hapless Molly screeched despairingly, her scolding tone beaten out of her. She rasped weakly. The sound rose higher and higher, and before any of us moved, it had stopped altogether. A few feathers floated earthward.

Matilda in this moment of stress was incoherent. She was the first to reach the yard, where she grabbed up a few stray brown feathers. The hawk was already out of sight.

"The beast! The—the beast!" It was as much as she could pronounce.

Beth had reached her by then, stretched out a hand to her floundering sister, thought better of it. For a moment she stood there empty-handed. Then her trick of explaining her sister asserted itself. She turned to us.

"It is hard to make you understand, I suppose, how terrible this is. Molly was so much—almost a person. We've been so alone here. And so, this, well. . . ."

That effort of Beth's to explain the situation finally aroused Matilda. She came at us fiercely, fairly shouting. She was oblivious of us, of course. Her quarrel was with that miserable hillside shack, with the years of dreariness. But she explained it better.

"Damnation! It was more than that! You make us seem like two old maids talking to ourselves. I say *no* to that and damn the notion! That hen was an idea. The idea of personal integrity. Standing alone and damn the consequences. Men try to live like that. Few do. Very few. The hen did. Did you see her? And this hawk, he's the witless brute force that insults us all. The best of us! We put ourselves above the beast, but when the hawk is hungry he comes for us. And what are we then?

"We liked Molly because we fancied ourselves her kind of a person. That's the truth of the matter. Birds of her feather! How do you like that?"

With an expression of disgust, she stopped short and snapped her head earthward, letting fall the few feathers which old Molly had lost in her fatal encounter.

I heard Anne's soft voice and when I looked up from a study of the ground at my feet, I saw that she had approached Matilda, put her hand out to her.

"Why don't you come home, to Connecticut? That's what you want to do, isn't it? Come home with me."

The sisters seemed to fold up at that. Perhaps it had been in their minds for a long time and they had never spoken of it aloud. Perhaps. I don't know. They seemed to get limp, Matilda and Beth together, and they slumped into chairs at the table. Neither spoke until they had sat reflecting for moments. Brittany, peasants on the mountain-side, the Bermuda sands, winter in the Connecticut hills—it must all have been in their minds. Perspiration poured down their faces without distracting their thought.

"But we couldn't," Matilda spoke her thought aloud. "We couldn't—any more than Molly could run from the hawk."

She spoke a great deal more, beginning slowly and reflectively. A little unsure of herself, it seemed, but gradually warming to the idea and adding intensity to her words. Soon she was glowing, her eyes looking at us brightly. Beth began to catch some of her conviction.

"Oh, we haven't given up. Only the other day we were talking about renting a place down in the valley where the soil is better. We saw a place we could get at a small rental."

Hours later, as the afternoon was cooling, we started home, Anne and I. The girls, by then, seemed cheerful and full of prospects.

Anne stirred one sceptic thought, however, which has stayed in my mind ever since. She said, "I wonder—was it worth it—if that's the way the West was settled?"

I don't like to carry that question around with me, but I confess it has lodged in my mind and I can't get rid of it.

Debt of Gratitude

▷ ▷ ▷ The town of Bear Paw was at the mouth of a canyon where the transcontinental railroad plunged into one of the many upheavals of the Rocky Mountains. It was proud of its situation and the slogan had been coined, "The Gateway City—Where Life Begins."

The town was spread on both banks of a fast mountain river, and it had rich houses and poor houses and churches, like any town. It was new, as age is reckoned among cities—a middle-aged man's life spanned its existence—but it had managed up to now to give birth to people and bury them and make misery for them in the interval.

Albert Smiley was one of the persons, just now, who was having his misery. It wasn't that he had any particular reason for living, but he was about to die, it seemed, and he wasn't ready to die.

His heart wouldn't go much further. It had practically stopped on him in the store and he had collapsed, while stepping across from the hardware department to the dry goods section. That was on Tuesday and today was Sunday—almost a week had passed.

The worst thing about dying was that he couldn't go to work at the store any more. It was thinking of that that braced him up; if he managed to live, in spite of the doctor shaking his head, it would be because of that. Anyhow, a man not yet sixty wasn't old.

The store was part of his digestion, and his sleep depended on it—
a man can't do the same thing for thirty-five years and not wear a trail
from going back and forth.

From this it should not be imagined that he owned the store.
Nothing of the sort. It belonged to Bear Paw's outstanding citizen. To
be the outstanding citizen one had to know the part, and play it.
Albert Smiley couldn't have done that, not in the way Ross Curzon
knew how to do it. People recognized that. To them Smiley was a
kind of grouch, a dried-up old man, a fellow who asked you what you
wanted when you came to the store.

But Mr. Curzon set people to nodding their heads, almost to lifting
their hats, when he passed in the street. A smile from him was as good
as finding money. Everybody knew his big white house, set back
among trees, with its columns across the front. On summer evenings
the townspeople walked down that way and listened to the music and
the voices coming through open windows. Those were just a few of
the things that went to making an outstanding citizen.

Albert Smiley lacked the qualifications, but people thought he
acted as if he owned the store just the same. His position there was
ambiguous, not even his fellow employees knew exactly what his
duties were. They knew that at one time he had managed the
hardware department, but a younger man was there now. He seemed
to have a kind of roving commission to poke his nose into any
department. Young clerks who defied him and asked where he got the
idea he could give orders got fired somehow. So the idea spread that
the old man was to be left alone.

It was Sunday morning, with death near, and Albert Smiley was
thinking of the store and Mr. Curzon.

He had become peevish after all these days in bed—he never had
been sick a day in his life. He would call his wife to his room every few
minutes and ask if she had sent for their son, why hadn't he come,
and wouldn't she call him again.

"Dear! Dear! Yes, yes! I'll call again."

Mrs. Smiley couldn't be impatient, knowing that Albert was at
death's door, as her mind phrased it, but she was getting terribly
upset. She was frightened every time he called and tried to get to him

before he should call a second time, for the extra effort might without warning carry him off—another phrase she had in mind.

She stood in the parlor and waited for their married son. "Hurry! Hurry!" she breathed.

Smiley's house was ordinary, more elaborate than young people were building nowadays, but ordinary. Beyond the verandah, with its pillars and railing, stretched a short lawn, and there were soft maples for shade. The kind of house no one looked at nowadays, but it had cost something in planning and effort and worry.

When Terence came he left his wife downstairs, hung his spring overcoat on the stair rail, and sprang for the stairs. He made it in three leaps. He had light hair and a pleasant face, and he smiled in the way young men smile when they have a good job, when they are just married, when nothing has gone wrong yet.

Terence's wife was young, too. He heard her telling his mother— "I'm sorry we took so long. We were just getting up when you called. Isn't it shameful!"

Smiley heard the young voice downstairs, heard his son's quick step at the door, then watched him approach the bed. The smile was fading as Terence went forward, giving way to a look of concern. Smiley's grey eyes missed none of it, but his lips remained still.

"How you feeling, Dad? We got here soon's we could."

Smiley waved to the chair.

His mouth was always pulled down at one corner in a harsh expression. People had called him dried-up and bad-tempered, sharp, nagging, and obstinate, but what they meant really was that he had an ugly mouth.

"Shall I tell Lois to come up now?"

Smiley shook his head. He had something to say to him alone.

It was April outside. The sound and smell and feeling of it were unmistakable. When you were waiting to die it didn't matter. You looked back over a long stretch, and you saw that of all the springs that had been, none had made any difference.

"I want you to get out of Curzon's store." Smiley began to talk only after he had seen the last of his son's smile fade out.

"I know you've got a good job there—better job already than me.

Boys get a better start nowadays. They go to college and take things easy at first, then when they start they get ahead of the old man in no time. That's all right. If I was starting I'd want to do it that way.

"You want to know why you're to quit Ross Curzon. . . ."

Terence knew what was to come—who that knew old Smiley didn't know his old grudge.

"People say I act like I own Ross Curzon's store. Well, I do. . . ."

It was a familiar beginning. Terence let himself slide lower in his chair and prepared himself for a full half hour of rewording an old story. There was a time, he could remember, when he had believed every word, and even now he didn't doubt but that the old man had some ground for grievance. But it wasn't as one-sided as his father made out. Mr. Curzon was really a fine fellow, one who had never failed in an obligation, as everybody knew, whose word was as good as his bond. Terence had learned these things for himself, but he never mentioned it. While his father talked he kept his eyes on the April scene through the window. He stretched his legs out and relaxed in that good young feeling of having a sure job and of being just married.

It seemed, according to the story, that Smiley had joined Ross Curzon right at the beginning, when the store had only one counter running lengthwise of the building and stuff piled up in every inch of space—nail kegs, buggy whips, bolted goods, flour, everything. Smiley was the first helper and when things went poorly, as they did most of the time at first, he drew no wages for months on end. But that was the least of the trouble.

Ross was drinking in those days and running around with women. His mind wasn't on business for five minutes together in any one day and he could have lost everything a hundred times over, if a different man had been in Smiley's place. He took care of Ross, hid the money when it came in and made sure it was used to pay the bills. He clerked and kept the books and swept the place out and stocked the shelves. And he nursed Ross, sobered him up whenever he could get hold of him, and sent the women about their business when they were trying to get their hands in Ross's pants pockets. He couldn't be around all the time, of course, and they got away with plenty. There were times when he wouldn't have given a nickel for the whole lay-out, it was that close to going on the rocks. No matter what happened later, it was Smiley who kept the business going right when it mattered. Ross had a lot of helpers later, but they weren't of any use to him then, because he didn't have them. That was what he wanted the world to realize.

The country grew up—nothing could stop that—and Ross's store grew right along with it. When mining played out, there was lumbering, and then farming came into its own. They began planting orchards and alfalfa in the Bitter Root Valley, and people began to have solid, regular incomes. The store went right along, new buildings were put up one after another, and instead of a trading post out from nowhere it became a regular plate glass museum spread over a city block.

Ross had left off drinking rather suddenly, about the time he got married, and he changed in other ways. He started going with a different crowd—no more dancing women and card players. His wife was the daughter of one of the first state senators and she brought along a string of politicians and their wives, people who lived a lot in Washington and Boston, and Ross got to going back East himself and even to Europe, and he stocked the store with fancy groceries and all manner of finery which his friends bought as part of their daily living. His wife got him to dressing in that fine way he had and she built that mansion down there—no one had ever seen a house as big as that around here—it was copied exactly from one of the New Orleans plantation places.

Smiley didn't realize right at first how Ross was changing. Nothing was ever said straight out that he wasn't to go on managing as always, but one day a slick-haired fellow from Boston showed up in the office and for a week Ross was showing him around and having private talks with him. Then Ross went off to Europe and didn't show up for several months. In that time the Boston fellow had turned everything upside down; he threw out stuff and had it sold at a fire sale; ripped out partitions and tore down shelves; had carpenters and painters and paper hangers running everybody crazy—and every time Smiley went rushing in to demand what the hell, the Boston fellow showed him a slip of paper, and sure enough it was Ross's orders.

After that Smiley was at sea for a long time. He tried to talk to Ross, but he couldn't pin him down to anything, couldn't even get in to him most of the time. Ross had learned tricks from that new crowd, and surrounded himself with girl secretaries and office boys and somebody was always stepping in front of you when you tried to get in to the office.

"Mr. Curzon is busy right now" or "Did you wish an appointment with Mr. Curzon? He will be occupied until tomorrow at 10:15." The damnest nuisance you could imagine.

And Ross wouldn't just say what was in his mind. "You're all right, Smiley, old fellow. There's a whale of a lot for you to do. Just dig in."

Like hell!

For a while he managed the hardware department. It had come to that. Instead of having the run of the whole store, he wound up with a single department. Of course one department did as much business in a month as the whole store used to do in a year, but it did seem like a come-down.

As it turned out, the hardware job didn't last, and that was what broke Smiley's heart. In less than a year he was out of it, not fired, he had never been told that he wasn't wanted. Ross sent in another man, another slick-haired fellow, "to help" in supervising the department and "perhaps make suggestions." The suggestions he made came so fast and were so upsetting to a man trying to keep a business running without changing things every day, that one or the other had to get out. Smiley went to Ross to speak his mind, but it was the same thing over again. The secretaries or the office boys popped up in his path and Mr. Curzon wasn't in.

Smiley went on. A secretary to the assistant manager would come to him with instructions to supervise a job in one of the warehouses, then after he'd been there for a few weeks an assistant secretary would come with further instructions.

So it came about that he had the run of the place, as a stray dog has the run of the town. Nobody claimed him, nobody wanted him, but he wasn't allowed to starve and so it was all right. And the peculiar thing was that throughout his decline in influence, his interest in the success of the store never faltered. He couldn't even lie down to die, because he couldn't get his mind off what he had helped to create.

Smiley didn't relate all the details that Sunday morning. They were known. But he said enough to make his meaning clear.

"Well, Ross cuts a fine figure in the world, now. I know he's got more to do than come to see me when I'm laying here. But where would his fine business be, where would he be, if I had let them chippies and tin-horn sports walk off with everything? And they were hungry enough to have done it, too.

"You see, son, it ain't no idle boast when I say I own Ross Curzon's store. I can't show no papers for it, but papers wouldn't make it any surer."

Then he came to a painful halt. He had just realized that his son wasn't listening, that he was gazing out the window and was a million miles away. Smiley felt himself tighten up inside. It had never occurred to him that his own family would come to act like other people when he told his story. He roused himself, tried to get rid of his frozen feeling.

"Terence!" He did get the boy to look at him.

"Terence. You see now why I don't want you to stay at Curzon's, don't you? It's been in my mind right along. You'll be smart if you go somewhere else, where they'll set more value by you in time to come."

Terence knew the answer but he hadn't the heart to say it. He sat up straight in his chair, pulled his legs in, then crossed them. That feeling of being young and having a good job, of being just married, made it difficult to talk to anyone worn out and dying and who had lost his place because he hadn't grown with the times.

"I'll go the minute I find something better, Dad. Don't worry about me."

Smiley held the silence.

"I don't just mean that. It ain't the bettering of yourself I mean. You'll do that easy enough. What I mean is to quit that man because of what he is. But I guess it's asking too much." He saw that it was and so he said it.

"Good jobs don't come every day, Dad."

"That's right, son."

"Well . . . Shall I tell Lois to come up now?"

Smiley felt himself freeze again, his heart paused painfully. The women folks might as well come.

It seemed that Mrs. Smiley and Lois had no sooner entered the room than the front door bell sounded its rusty clatter.

Mrs. Smiley straightened nervously. Sudden noises set her to fluttering these days. She patted the collar of her dress into place and went downstairs.

Upstairs they heard her exclaim: "Why, Mr. Curzon! Why. . . . How do you do! Come in!"

Terence's glance went from his father to Lois, and Lois looked from father to son. Smiley flushed. His gaze held straight ahead.

Curzon had learned the part. He came in freshly ironed and pressed, with suede gloves, flower in his lapel, and bowler hat in hand. No one not playing the part of the outstanding citizen would dare appear in such dress in Bear Paw.

As he walked through Smiley's house he involuntarily lowered his head, as if he were going through a low-ceilinged cabin. He climbed the shrieking stairs without displaying any discomfort.

He paused in Smiley's bedroom door. Terence and Lois, as one, rose to their feet, and Curzon gave them an acknowledging glance. Then his face returned to the expression of concern which had gathered there as he mounted the stairway.

"I'm grieved, Albert. Terribly grieved."

Smiley watched him advance, as though through a cloud. But it wasn't really a cloud. It was a dimly lit interior—a long room, with a counter running down one side—odors came next—kerosene, bacon, greased harness.

"Morning, Ross. See you made it." The words suited the long, dim room and a time of long ago.

"Yes, Albert. I made it fine!" Ross Curzon laughed a little at words which were vaguely familiar. Then he brushed them away. "Well! I've got something for you here, Albert. But let me tell you something first."

He held the small package in his open hand and had everyone gazing fixedly at it as he talked.

"I called our directors together on Thursday, Albert, and had a heart-to-heart talk about you. You'd have blushed to hear some of the things I said about you. I know what you were worth to me, to the store, during those early years. I haven't forgotten. They were tough times, and we took the bumps together. Just the two of us in those days and it kept us hustling. But we were bound to get ahead, and we did. And today the Curzon store owes you a debt of gratitude.

"I spoke of these things to the directors and we agreed to acknowledge our indebtedness in fitting form. Something to express what you can't get into words.

"Mrs. Smiley, won't you do me the honor of undoing the package, and we'll see what they've sent Albert."

The fingers fumbled at the ribbon.

"Oh, dear! A watch! A beautiful watch! Look, Albert!"

"Yes, Albert. It is a rare Swiss movement. There is nothing better made. And the case itself is a beautiful thing. Our most valuable employee, and we honor ourselves in honoring him. You'll find that sentiment engraved inside the case."

Then, before leaving, after everyone had examined the trophy, Mr. Curzon spoke his final word.

"You've earned your rest, Albert. Hereafter, your salary will be continued as in the past, but you're to take it easy. Rest and enjoy yourself, perhaps travel a bit, it will do you good. But no more work, I'll ask Mrs. Smiley to see to that."

He looked kindly upon Mrs. Smiley, gave a paternal blessing to Terence and his wife, and withdrew.

Everyone felt it, so it couldn't have been pure imagination—but it did seem as if the room had been changed by Mr. Curzon's visit; it seemed brighter, a pleasant odor lingered, something was different.

Or perhaps Smiley didn't think so. He handled the watch, studied it, but his attention was not altogether on it. He looked at it, and beyond it. The others checked the words they would have uttered. They waited.

They wanted to say something in praise of Mr. Curzon, of his coming in person, of his friendliness, of his doing the right thing.

Smiley looked at each one, looking for something he would not find. When he was satisfied of that, he spoke, tiredly. "I don't begrudge him his getting ahead. I guess he deserves it as much as another. He's a good man for you to stay with, Terence. Probably as good a man as you'll ever find, all things considered."

The Wedding Night

▷ ▷ ▷   There was a gay dance at Francis du Montier's ranch in the foothills. It was the wedding night and the wedding dance of du Montier's daughter Angelique, called Babe, who had taken as husband a certain Forrest Stevens, a stranger in the country.

First snow had fallen just a week before and the hills and valley sparkled under a clear moon.

The du Montier house was famous for its dances. It was a large house, built of hewn logs, and the dance floor ran across the entire front. The du Montiers, those of the family who were still able-bodied, were a volatile, noisy, impulsive lot, with inexhaustible energy for carousing and gay-living—as those words were understood in that corner of Montana jack-pine hills.

Old Francis himself looked on at the dance. His bed was shoved off into one corner of the dance floor. There he sat, or lay, with a chair and pillow under his back. He watched everything that went on in his house, without making a gesture. When he spoke no one listened. He was paralyzed.

Francis had been a big man, but the gnawing of time had made away with most of what his frame contained and left him hollow. His voice resembled a dribble of water sounding in a cave.

It was a gay dance. The revelry had begun at sundown and would continue until daybreak at least. The dancers, gay devils, had already eaten one meal; soon they would have another.

Hector Marengeau, a du Montier relative, called the dances. There was no one who could equal him in the art of making people gay. He shouted and clapped his hands and jigged and even danced on his hands, without missing a beat. He left no blanks in his calling. As each figure was being carried through he filled in the interval with droll expressions.

". . . Swing that girl, the pretty little girl, the girl you left behind you! She's slim around the waist and pretty in the face and just the girl to mind you. . . ."

So the dance went. A man would shout as he swung the "pretty little girl" until her feet left the floor, and the "pretty little girl" would scream with ecstasy. The fiddles played shrill and fast.

The bride was the gayest of all, as could be expected. The men clamored for one wild dance with Babe du Montier. They filled the room with their shouts and laughter. They clapped their hands and stomped their feet until at times the fiddles sounded quite weak and plaintive.

She was a girl of spirit, a true du Montier. There was bursting energy in every gesture of her small body. She had grey eyes and black hair and the combination seemed to stir men. Everything about her seemed to stir men, so that she was never alone wherever she might be. Some fellow was always with her, stumbling over things as he walked at her side and laughing loudly.

"I don't ask them to follow me. I don't even look at them." That was what she used to say to the Sister Superior at the convent school. Her stay there was not long. The school was too near her home for the peace of mind of the Sister Superior. It had become impossible to take the girls out for walks on Sunday afternoons. Boys would come riding on the wildest horses they could find and dash back and forth until the girls were frightened out of their wits. All but Babe. She would seem to understand what was happening and of course it amused her.

So it was when she returned from school. Men always acted as if they were riding wild horses when they were around her. She looked at them and laughed, but denied that she had anything to do with their behavior.

It was a gay dance, all right. The fiddlers couldn't go fast enough. The old ladies sitting on chairs and benches around the room were in hilarious mood; children scooted between the feet of the dancers. The kerosene lamps flared up and down as a skirt swished through the air. The big stove in the corner had been filled with pine knots and the heat seared one's face.

Old Francis, propped up in bed, watched all this. Sometimes he dozed, but he would soon be awake and watching, as before, with expressionless face. Dancers who jarred his bed said not a word to him.

There was one other who did nothing but look on—this was the bridegroom, Forrest Stevens. He stood in the doorway leading into the kitchen, a strange figure at such a gathering. None of the St. Xavier people knew how to take him. Many a look and grin was sent in his direction, especially from those men who made a nest around Babe; some laughed right out.

"What d'you make of him?" the question went round. "He's kind of a boob, ain't he?"

"All I know's the old lady's took a fancy to him. They say it's 'cause he tipped his hat first time he saw her."

"Ha! Ha! He tipped his hat to her! Ha! Ha!"

Forrest was a handsome boy—tall, slender, with blue eyes and a wave in his hair, like a picture boy; but it was easy to see that he had never enjoyed himself much. He stood near the doorway watching the dancers, a strange look of confusion in his eyes.

"Look at him gawk!"

"Just stands there like a—like a. . . ."

"It beats me. It's a puzzler. Where did she find him?"

The bride herself was none too easy on him. She would leave a man's arms as she danced by and go up to Forrest. She had a bold, mocking smile which he could not meet without looking uneasy.

"My darling! You must learn to dance. Tomorrow, I'll show you how it goes. Why don't you go talk to *mama* in the kitchen? Darling, don't stare at me that way! I'll think you don't love me. Run along, *mon brave*."

The onlookers listened closely, then glanced at each other. It was incredible. How that Babe could twist a man around her little finger!

"It's a shame! And him such a nice boy!" The women shook their heads. It was too much for them.

The bridegroom disappeared.

"What I don't see," one fiddler remarked over his partner's shrill scraping, "is why the hell she married such a—such a. . . ."

His partner winked. "They say he tips his hat to the old girl. It starches her tail feathers."

▽

How had it happened? He had asked himself the question suddenly, for the first time, in church that morning. It was as he approached the altar railing with his bride, Angelique du Montier. She had looked up at him, in that bold way she had, and he had to look away. How had it happened?

At that moment, he remembered, he should have been at the Wesleyan College, completing his theological course. He should have been preparing for service under the Board of Foreign Missions. In India, China, where his father had been. His classmates were going their usual ways; they had already forgotten him. He had fallen by the way. Unaccountably. The routine which a year ago had seemed tedious and inevitable, now struck him as being out of his reach, lost to him.

How had it happened? The moment of confusion endured until he had been made one with his bride. The Angelique who then looked up shyly, with a suggestion of tear film in her eyes, she brought ease to his heart. It was this girl who had hung softly in his arms a week ago, avoiding his eyes, murmuring: "You're a fine boy, Forrest. You're too good for my kind. Why don't you go away and forget me?" It was to her (not to the bold smile) that he could swear: "My beloved! You will make me good! You will purify me!" It was in full faith.

He remembered that, as she turned from the railing and looked softly upon him. And the question which had come so rudely upon him a short while before was dissolved in the smoke of the acolyte's censer.

▽

In the kitchen Babe's mother, Agnes, had her own circle—women whose tongues wagged in bitter mouths. They sat by the stove on which coffee and pots of food were sending up clouds of steam. The women mumbled on tirelessly, and no one joined the group. Once during the evening a young half-breed, quite drunk, staggered up to Agnes.

"What d'you mean marrying Babe to this—this. . . . Ain't the valley boys good enough? Maybe they was too good. . . ."

Without a word, Agnes advanced with a piece of stove wood in her hand, and the impudent fellow retreated.

"Get out of here!" she said, and that was enough. She was a good du Montier, too.

The old ladies at the stove exchanged glances during the scene. When Agnes returned to her seat, Martha Dowd, a bleary-eyed woman with a black shawl over her shoulders, leaned forward.

"Your Babe thinks a lot of this fellow, don't she?" The others waited expectantly.

Agnes sneered at the question. "You think Babe ain't straight with the young fellow. You think she's played him a trick, maybe. We'll see."

Forrest was entering the kitchen as Agnes rose to go for him. He had just been turned out of the dance room by Babe. Agnes looked proud of her possession as she guided him to her companions at the stove. She drew up a chair for him and brought whisky and glasses from a cupboard.

"Drink to my son!" she taunted her companions. "Such a quiet boy, smart too, and clean you can be sure. I said my girl would never marry a breed. I been saying it ever since I borne her, and there you are. Was I as good as my word? This good looking fellow comes along last fall. . . . He was selling us a book, Martha Dowd. It's in there on the center table now. What was the name of the book, son?"

"It was *The Family Book of Familiar Quotations from the Classic and Modern Authors*. I was selling it to pay my last year in college." As Forrest spoke he watched Agnes' sharp eyes for the sign that should tell him whether his words were agreeable or not. He had been doing this ever since he had known her.

"Wasn't that nice! He was going to college. How would you like that for your girl, Martha?" The question was not meant to be answered and Agnes hurried on. "But the very next week he came back with a buggy-load of books and wanted to stay with us while he peddled them.

The first time he came he only had one book and he showed it to people and they bought it. So the next time he had to have books for everybody. Well, he and Babe took to each other, which was something new for Babe. Usually she don't take to strangers. When his books was gone he just stayed."

Forrest's staring eyes raised slowly to Agnes' face and his mouth opened.

"You invited me, Mrs. du Montier." He spoke hurriedly, correcting a false impression.

"I did? Well, s'pose I did! I could see you wanted it though you was afraid to say so. I know how it is with you quiet boys. But tell us what you think of my girl. We was just saying what a bu-u-tiful couple you make. Here, take your whisky."

Forrest took the whisky in a single throw, and for a moment his face burned crimson as he fought against strangulation. He managed not to cough.

"Don't be so bashful," she teased.

"I guess I never loved a girl before. When you told me Angelique would like to marry me, I couldn't understand it. I didn't know what it was—I mean to be in love. . . ."

"Son, what are you talking about?" Agnes scowled, then smiled. "You love my girl, don't you? Because if you don't it's time I was finding out. . . ."

Forrest was like a talking machine with a set piece to play and he went on without answering Agnes' imperative questioning.

"I went home to tell father. I wanted him to know that a girl was in love with me and wanted me to marry her. We live alone, you know, since Mother died, and I have always told him my plans. It was too much for him. I was afraid it might be. He has had a weak heart since he returned from field work in India. It was evening when I told him, and he said he couldn't discuss it. He just went off to bed. In the morning he complained of his heart. I called the doctor and came away. I had promised Angelique to be back the next day."

There was a stirring among the old women, elbows were pressed against neighboring sides. Heads half turned. Agnes ignored these sly movements.

"Well, you ran away for my girl! I guess that shows what he thinks of her, eh Martha? Babe will be a good wife to you. I could tell you liked her pretty well."

Agnes' friends had listened complacently, smiling their company smiles. But curiosity ate at their innards and caused them to squirm under Agnes' skillful maneuvering. Martha Dowd finally could not endure it and asked a question on her own account.

"They say you was to be a preacher. Is that so?" Her mouth was so puckered with smiling that she had difficulty in speaking.

The acrid atmosphere of battle which filled the room was not lost even upon him. He must be careful of what he said, if he meant to be on friendly terms with Agnes.

"Father's plans were not always my own." His polite smile baffled Martha Dowd. She did not try another question.

Agnes looked pleased. "Come along. I ought to talk to you." She led Forrest out of the kitchen and sat down with him at the foot of the stairway, which rose out of the hall in the middle of the house. There they could see the dancers whirling by.

"Those old women want to stick their noses in. Don't mind 'em, son."

There was a pause, then a moment of sweet smiling. "Son, there's one thing I want to say first off—don't never tell nobody I asked you to marry my girl. It sounds bad. Folks will think you got no gumption of your own. See?"

Hector Marengeau was calling a dance. . . . "She's got a big upper lip like the rudder of a ship, and her nose has the whistle of a steamboat too. . . ."

Agnes continued. "Tell me, why ain't you been dancing, like the rest? Can't you dance?"

"No. My folks didn't believe in dancing, so I never learned."

In the darkness he found it easier to talk. His attention was not so firmly held, to the confusion of his thoughts, by her bright eyes. His life had been modeled on repose, soft speech, quiet ways, and his understanding depended on them.

"That's all right for them that think that way. A quiet man's a fine thing in this world. I haven't had any trouble with my Francis since he had his stroke. But don't be too quiet, not with that Babe of mine. You want to learn to dance, step around. She expects it."

After a long pause she leaned forward and asked in a heavy whisper:

"Have you been out with girls? Do you know how to come round them?"

"Come round them?" he echoed. The note of absurd innocence enraged Agnes, though she did not show it.

"Just listen to me, son. Mind what I say. A girl's no lily flower, don't forget it. D'you know what I mean? I mean that for all their doll faces and innocent airs—it's all seeming. We say the men are hot after the girls, but it's the girls are hot for men, only they make it show up the other way about. Did you learn that in school?"

He shook a wondering head, his lips opening to an unvoiced "No."

"You didn't learn it in books and you didn't learn it from the little girls you was brought up with! It must a been a dead place where you lived. What was the use going to college and being a preacher if you didn't learn that much before you got there? It's a wonder!

"You follow my advice and you'll be a better man for it. My Babe, now, is like all the girls who've got fellows on the brain. They want straightenin' out, and a mother can't do it, not if she used a horse-whip. There's just an amount of hot feelings in them that's got to be put up with until you get them settled. I'm talking straight out to you because you wouldn't know what I meant otherwise. Your pa, instead of fainting when you told him you was getting married, might a talked sense to you."

Forrest was blinking and looking upon Agnes with fascinated gaze. He could not account for the chills which her blunt words sent through his blood.

"I'm not saying Babe is any better or any worse than the others. But people have got it in their heads that she's a good for nothing. Those old hens around the stove are taking her to pieces this minute. I don't want you to believe a word of it. They're troublemakers. Well, I'm sick and tired of it and from now on I'm leaving it up to you."

"What do you want me to do, Mrs. du Montier?" he asked, with a front of determination.

"Why, just this—take her to bed and be a man with her." The words were not without a smile.

His front collapsed. "I—I'm. I see."

"You shouldn't leave her alone in there. Ain't you got no feelings for her?"

He protested hurriedly that he did have feelings, but that he didn't dance and he doubted if she'd be willing to leave off dancing. After all, she was free to enjoy herself. He did not mind. He would do anything for her. It made Agnes snort.

"This is what you got to do. When the next dance stops, go in there, shove those fellows off and make her go with you. Talk to her. Show her you got feelings."

"But. . . ."

"There's no buts in this business. You got to show her how it is. She'll be with other men if you don't stop her. She's just a girl and you got to take care of her."

"I see. I've got to take care of her," he repeated vacuously. "What should I say when I go up to her?"

"Take her by the waist and say, 'Come on, dearie, the dance is over.' You ought to be able to figure out that much."

"I'll say, 'Come along. I have something to tell you.' "

"Put it to her strong."

Agnes took his arm and walked him to the door of the dance room.

There was only one fiddler playing, the other had gone outside to look at the stars. The lamps flared up and down more quietly. The dancers were tiring, a few were dozing in their chairs. But not Babe. One would have thought she was just beginning.

"Now!" Agnes whispered. "Let's see you do something." She pushed him into the room. He blinked and bumped into an approaching couple.

There was no denying that he was a charming boy, though that was not the way Agnes thought of him. The word she used was "clean." She told everyone "He's a clean boy," and by that she meant, for one thing, that he had blond hair, a rare sight in that country of French-Canadians and Indians.

Old Francis lay awake, his eyes staring at the ceiling from sheer exhaustion of watching the dancers. Forrest walked carefully around the dancers toward the bed. People shouted to him and slapped him on the back as he passed.

"You oughta wear your hat and tip it to the ladies!" someone was saying.

"Agnes hid his hat so he can't, except to her."

Francis rolled his head and watched Forrest. Perhaps he understood that this was his son-in-law. There was no expression on his face. His eyes were grey, like Babe's.

Forrest was not looking at Francis. He stood watching the dancers and chewing his lip. Then he started forward.

Approaching Babe, he looked anxiously for that softness in her eyes which he had seen that morning at the church, and on one other occasion. He was hoping desperately that she would not give him instead that look of boldness and mocking which he could not face. His eyes besought this, but she, whether she understood or not, was in no soft mood. She called out:

"Hello, old man! Coming for a dance? My feet are tired."

There was an implication in her words which Forrest did not sense. The dancers paused, curious.

"I want to tell you something. The dance is over, dearie. I want to tell you something. You look tired."

"Me tired? That's a good one! Is that all?"

"No. I want to tell you something. Let's go upstairs."

Someone snickered. Babe blushed.

"What do you mean? If you want to go to bed, go on up. I'll be around tomorrow sometime."

He would have let it go at that, but it was too late to stop. He stepped up close to Babe and slipped his arm partway round her waist. He was not recalling Agnes' suggestion of using force. The action was involuntary, part of the impulse to go on.

"Come on. You've had enough dancing. We'll go upstairs."

Babe looked amazed and drew back for a moment. He reached out to take hold of her again.

"You damned fool!" she blazed at him. She slapped his face. "Insult me, before everybody!"

The crowd drew back in amazement. The room fell silent. Those who had been drowsing came to life and blinked their eyes. Then, from the doorway, Agnes laughed. Her face, visible a moment before, disappeared. Babe turned and walked to the other end of the room.

The boy was startled by what he saw, seemingly for the first time. The crowd appalled him, and from long habit he held himself motionless, thinking in that way to attract less attention. It was the only way he knew of conducting himself before others.

In the silence of the moment, Old Francis coughed gently, but it sounded as loud as a stamping foot. Forrest turned, relieved that something had occurred to divert attention from himself. Francis was watching his son-in-law, and when he spoke his voice sounded like water dripping in a cave.

"Better go 'way, stranger. Don' you know . . . you're a blind for the wild ones . . . you're a tame duck . . . set out for the high-flyers. . . . It's all lies. . . ."

The redness was ebbing from Forrest's face. People looked at him, grinned, then turned away. They pressed forward to enter the kitchen, where Babe had gone to join her mother. No one wanted to be around the bridegroom. They had become uncomfortable in his presence. Soon he was alone in the room. Francis was asleep, at least feigning sleep.

In these first moments, Forrest Stevens might have laughed, or wept, but what he did was to stare at the wall lamps. The flames were quiescent now, burning steadily, and in their repose was some quality that appealed to his understanding.

Newcomers

▷ ▷ ▷   A newcomer sets people to talking and acting queerly. If they want to learn the stranger's name, they ask him how he likes the weather up their way. If they've heard that he's been married and divorced three times and want to find out about it, they say "It's sure hell how we don't get enough rain in summer to wash a man's back."

The newcomer usually is a queer one, too. When a question is put to him, he looks as if he had been hit on the head. He mumbles as if talking in his sleep.

At least, it used to be that way in Montana.

Frank Barnes and his family, when they came into the country, upset everybody because they had a different way of doing things. They were Easterners, of course, and college people too, and that seemed to explain some of their ways.

"We're practical people," Frank Barnes would say, in explanation of why he imported six registered jersey milch cows instead of buying out of a local herd of mixed breeds—but the explanation explained nothing. Expensive, imported cattle always took sick; you couldn't count on such animals. Local people all knew that.

They talked a lot about "practical" things. They hadn't been in the country three days when Mrs. Barnes was heard to say that something "practical" ought to be done about the Indians. By that she meant that somebody ought see to it that Indian children got milk to drink. They had never lived next door to an Indian Reservation before, and so they couldn't have known that Indian children never drank milk.

But these things happened later. The Barneses had been doing surprising things from the beginning.

There had been a section of land lying idle for several years in the Crow Creek district—that was dryland farming country, where men plowed and sowed and in the fall of the year charged it all up to the storekeeper and the bank; and the storekeeper and the bank people, being tender-hearted, didn't mind. This section of land had been idle for several years, until one day a motortruck with canvas-covered trailer, a kind of *de luxe* covered wagon, pulled out of the road and drew up alongside the squat, unpainted farm buildings which had become almost lost in a jungle of weeds.

There was a ranch house across the road, and a second one a half-mile farther along. The house across the way—it was Jim Davis' place—was the first to act.

The truck arrived just after noon and for a while nothing much happened. One could guess that the newcomers were eating a cold lunch, stretching cramped legs and saying "Well, we're here!" An hour later everybody in the family was tugging and lifting and carrying. They could be counted then: man; woman; thirteen-year-old girl, judged by her long, thin legs; ten–eleven-year-old boy; a five-year-old, at first taken for a girl in overalls but later discovered to be a boy with yellow hair, and a baby that got lost and got hurt all through the afternoon.

In midafternoon Mrs. Jim Davis sent over her girl Daisy—a pug-nosed, saucy adolescent, who came looking very solemn. Her face had been washed and she had put on a freshly starched dress for just this errand, one could tell.

"Ma says," her message went, "if you'll wait till Pa comes from the field, he'll help you with the stove." She gasped there and had to swallow fast to get out the rest of her message before she was interrupted. "If you want to cook something hot before the stove gets set you can come to our house and welcome."

The newcomer's wife had waited, smiling. "We're the Barneses.

We've come to take the Blodgett place." She was surprisingly calm and forthright about saying who they were. "Tell your mother thank you so much. We haven't any really heavy stuff. We use an oil stove for summer cooking, so you see. . . ."

They were all friendly. Indeed, Daisy took back the information that they were very nice people. They didn't look like farmers, but they were nice. She had been introduced to all of them, including a girl her own age named Sadie. And no, they didn't need any help. They hadn't brought any heavy stuff. They cooked on an oil stove in summer—and didn't that make the food taste? And what did they mean, they hadn't brought any *heavy* stuff? It sounded like camping out.

$$\triangledown$$

When the newcomers, that is the Barneses, had been settled a few weeks, they were asked over to Sunday dinner by the Cramers, who had the ranch half a mile down the road. The Davises would be there, too; a neighborly gathering.

It was in fact a community gathering by the time everybody arrived. The spring seeding was about completed and men were feeling that they could stand to have a Sunday off, having been going steadily at plowing and one thing after another for a month. An hour before the early afternoon dinner Carlson and his family had arrived; old man Wheatley and his wife were there; and there was another family of newcomers, the young Hoggetts and their infant, who were so far from any neighbors that they had been slighted by the community and were now being made up to.

No one cared much about the Hoggetts, the other newcomers. They were the kind of people about whom you could learn all you wanted to know by just looking at them. Both were tall and thin; both looked sour and acted as if they felt like they looked; both whined in their noses, and they were always in bad luck. People are careful how they act around their sort, for fear of inviting familiarity.

But Frank and Mamie Barnes were a different sort. Whatever peculiarities they might have, at least they were substantial. It had become known by then that they had just come from ten years of managing the grain crop on the biggest ranch in the state—one of those show-off places owned by a grossly rich Easterner who didn't know a badger hole from the Grand Teton. It was reasoned that Barnes must have made good money on a job like that. He might even be a relative by marriage of the rich Easterner. Rich people kept things in the family, it was said.

Farm management on a place like that was reported to be all scientific. They weighed what went into a cow and what came out of her; they planted oats and alfalfa together, and after a few years they plowed up the alfalfa (seed costing what it did, too) and planted wheat. It was a wonder they ever knew what was going to sprout when spring came. Frank Barnes was that kind of a farmer, then. He had learned it in a college back East.

When the Barneses arrived just before one o'clock, with their thirteen-year-old Sadie, eleven-year-old Buck, five-year-old Morton (the one who had been taken for a girl the first day), and Baby Frank, a great flurry resulted. The women were all starched up and their hair pinned tightly; the men perspired in wool serge suits.

Mrs. Ben Cramer, the hostess, big and jolly and breathing in a heavy, masculine sort of way, rushed from the kitchen wiping her hands on the front of her over-all apron. "You just sit down, Mrs. Barnes, and we'll have a snack in a minute. Kathleen!" she shouted for the girl standing at her elbow. "See what you can find for the player piano. I'm sure Miss Sadie would like to hear some music. The young folks do like to have music going. Well, Mrs. Barnes, it's real nice to have you—just sit down now."

"Not at all!" Mrs. Barnes had been meeting the ladies with a nod and making them feel at home. "I won't have you doing all the work and me sitting by. We're practical people, Mrs. Cramer. I'm more used to an apron than party dresses."

Her talking about practical people brought smiles, but she won the good will of all the ladies. Mamie Barnes was all right. Nothing stand-offish about her. They liked the fact that her hands showed that they had peeled vegetables and hung clothes out in windy weather. They liked her matter-of-factness. There was nothing helpless about her.

While such notions were being conceived in the house, the men outdoors were proceeding with a game of their own. It consisted first in sitting, standing and leaning in various angles on the front porch, then in going off to look around the lot: at the hogs, the calves (a man never showed off the chickens unless he had a lot of fancy hens and fancy trap nests), the tool shed, and the barn.

They were solemn about it. They held gates open for each other. They walked rather stiff-legged. Ben Cramer was in a sweat trying to keep the talk going; it was like running to get a kite up when there wasn't any wind. Ben usually had a lot to say about hogs and calves and growing crops, but then he wasn't usually talking to a man who was accustomed to planting twenty thousand acres of wheat every year (that was what they had heard). What would Barnes care about a forty-acre patch of fall wheat coming up spotty? Out of habit he might say, "Plow her under!" and it was a man's money crop for the year.

Jim Davis sensed his neighbor's troubled thoughts and tried to help him out. Davis was a long, rail-splitter kind of man with a reputation for the stories he told. He tried a few. He had one in particular that never failed. It was supposed to get funnier the more you thought about it. He tried it.

"It seems there was a man had a cork leg and he got married and didn't want the wife to know about it. So he says to her they'd have to sleep with a sheet between them. And the wife says well she didn't mind straining some things, but she wasn't going to start with having strained relations."

Ben Cramer laughed like a good neighbor; old man Wheatley guffawed; Carlson looked stunned for a moment, then made a sound like a whinnying horse; Hoggett, who didn't matter at any rate, grunted. But Frank Barnes just looked kind of sick. He must have heard it before, or maybe it was too strong for him. They couldn't tell.

At the hog pen Barnes stood with hands in pocket and failed to say that the hogs were fat or good looking or what were they fed. He didn't give Ben a chance. At the calf pasture he leaned against a fence post and seemed to get dreamy. There wasn't the least indication of what he was thinking.

By the time the barn had been gone over the conductors of the tour began to look foolish. They would have to join the women folks with everybody solemn and staring off into space. And they would have to explain to the wives afterward. They were passing through the feeding alley and were about to leave by the rear door where the manure was carried out. As Ben Cramer came to the last stall he reached into the manger, pushed aside the hay that lay there, and came up with a gallon jug. It was his last strategem. The way things were going, he would probably discover that the newcomer taught temperance in a Sunday school.

"I hope none of you boys object to taking a nip on a Sunday?" He knew his neighbors' principles. Only one person needed to answer.

Barnes looked at the gallon jug, then at Cramer. Whatever had been weighing upon his mind must have been jolted. His eyes flickered.

"Where did that come from?"

Cramer pointed to the stall and was ready to carry it back. His look was of one caught in mischief.

"Man! And you've been wasting time taking us to see the hogs!"

Everybody had to sit down and just laugh. Davis said it was the funniest thing he'd ever heard; and Cramer said well the joke was on him and they would have to drink on it.

Barnes had become a different person to all of them. He had a sense of humor, that was what. When he sat down and took off his hat they could see him better. He was sun and windburned like the rest of them. Even if he had learned farming in a college, his hands had raspy surfaces when he rubbed them together, which showed that he had taken hold of things and knew how to work.

When they had had about three drinks around and were beginning to feel the kinks disappear from their backbones somebody discovered that Barnes' boy, the one called Buck, was with them. The men fell silent. They did not want to encourage the boy, in case his father wanted to get rid of him. They waited for Frank to act. They thought, of course, that he would get a serious tone in his voice and ask the boy if they were ready to eat, or where were the other kids. Barnes surprised them.

"Hello, Buck! How would you like a drink of Ben's corn whisky?"

The boy was not abashed, and that surprised the men as much as Frank's unexpected way of greeting him. The father might be slightly drunk and that would account for him, but the boy seemed to be used to such familiarities. He wasn't more than twelve, but from his manner he might have been going around with a moustache.

Ben Cramer made a motion toward the boy. "You mean to let him have a drink, Frank?" By then they had become Frank and Ben and Jim; old man Wheatley was Dad; the cotton-headed Carlson was Swede, and Hoggett turned out to be Ned.

"Why not? Will you get silly if we give you a drink, Buck?" He seemed to think it unnecessary to ask his son such a question.

"I guess not. That drink you gave me at Christmas didn't make me silly, did it?"

Cramer was still worried. "You know how the women are. They got their own notions. I keep this jug out in the barn just so there won't be no questions asked. You don't suppose the boy will tell, do you?"

Barnes resented that. He had a better opinion of his son. "Hell, no! When you know Buck you'll appreciate him better. We know lots of things between us that the women folks never hear about. The men stick together in our family."

The men laughed, not knowing exactly what to make of it. From the first they had suspected that Frank Barnes was a rich man. Now they were beginning to feel sure of it. Only rich men and their sons could be so free and easy. That's the way it was with rich people, they understood. It made them a little uneasy.

Up at the house, after much discussion, the women had set a separate table for the children in one corner of the room, rather than make them wait until their elders had eaten. It was kind of mean, Mamie Barnes said and the others agreed, to make them wait, because generally the kids were hungrier than the grown-ups. They feel it stronger, they said. Cramers' Kathleen, Davis' Daisy, and Sadie Barnes, who had become as thick as molasses, were making a lark out of setting the children's table and waiting on it. The three of them were in high color over the prospect of their new friendship. Each time their eyes met they looked kind of nervous and pent-up. They seemed to have long stories they wanted to tell each other.

The men came in like a March wind, scattering hats and coats around and blowing with good fellowship. They had washed their hands and faces long ago and since they hadn't been doing anything they were ready to eat. They had got started on the price of wheat just before entering the house and were trying to draw out Barnes. There was a subject he ought to know like a book. But Barnes switched the talk when they entered the room where the women stood waiting.

"Mrs. Cramer," he said in that sober way which they now recognized to be witty, "you can always tell the opinion a woman has of her men folk by the table she sets for them. We ought to feel flattered. You've got enough here to feed an army."

It was true. There was hardly a piece of white tablecloth showing, so thickly were the dishes and bowls massed together. It needed a strong appetite to face the battery.

"It's all good, plain food, Mr. Barnes. I like to see a man eat hearty." Mrs. Cramer was slightly agitated. There was something funny intended by the way he said that, but she couldn't stop to figure it out.

Mrs. Barnes soothed her. "Frank isn't delicate, Mrs. Cramer. I've seen him outsit a table full of threshers. And he's never serious, except about wheat growing."

Husbands and wives became aware at the same moment that the Barneses were looking at each other. The women were waiting for that flash of steel or that sugared warning to tread with care which they always expected to see when married people looked at each other in company; and the men, still not knowing what to make of Frank Barnes, looked for that tamed expression which would signify that he shared the common lot where wives were concerned. But neither wives nor husbands saw what they were looking for. The Barneses, exchanging glances, gave an intimate glimpse of each other which was as surprising as anything they had yet said or done. Their eyes hid no monsters. The men were the first to look away.

Then there was the meal to eat. Dishes passed and were scooped of their contents; heaped loads on fork or knife made the quick trip to gaping mouths; deep draughts of milk or coffee washed it away.

The talk finally got around to Frank Barnes' job on Cornelius Ryan's show-place ranch across the mountains—Cornelius Ryan being the grossly rich Easterner who, it was said, kept the place so he would have room enough for his summer guests. The stories they had heard of its bigness were true, after a fashion. It wasn't twenty thousand acres of wheat they planted; it wasn't ten trainloads of cattle they shipped each year; it wasn't a hundred miles from the front gate to the ranch house—Frank Barnes smiled at the questions. It was a big ranch just the same. Yes, he had been manager of the grain crop, and was damned glad to be out of it. Barnes said this strongly.

"It's all very well to work with good tools and have a free hand— but rich men have a way of thinking they buy you body and soul when they hire you. You're either one of them, or you're a flunkey. Mamie and I are too good democrats for that, aren't we?"

Again there was an exchange of friendly glances between the Barneses, and those at table almost stopped eating. What did being a democrat have to do with giving up a job like that? A lifetime job! Wait until Frank Barnes had to pay his own bills for seed wheat and threshing! He might decide, then, that it wasn't so bad, being next to a rich man.

Until then, the grown-ups had paid no attention to the children. The older girls were seeing to the filling of plates and to cautioning against hoggish manners. Only when talk got drowned out at the grown-up table were the young ones hushed by their mothers.

There had been that lull after Frank Barnes expressed himself about working for rich men, and he had made it more confusing by adding a moment later: "This country was meant for the common folks. We wanted to get away from lords and landed proprietors, but it seems we have them with us just the same. I don't care for the breed myself." The men cracked their heads trying to figure it out. A while ago they had been thinking that Barnes must be rich because of the easy way he had with his family. Now, they were stumped. If it wasn't money that made people that way, what was it? The women were thinking about incomes too. They were wondering how much the Barneses were accustomed to spend in a year and how they could stretch their own incomes in order to buy a few extras. There had been that thought-taking silence, and then they heard what made every one sit stiff with expectancy.

The twelve-year-old Buck, with whisky fuming in his head, had turned argumentative. His sister Sadie had tried to squelch him, unsuccessfully. When she or Daisy or Kathleen came by to serve him, he pinched their legs. The devil was in him. Then that silence fell, and his voice suddenly rose up in argument. He was answering something that had been said.

"Cat's sake! That ain't nothing! My dad and me know lots of things we don't tell the women! The men folks stick together in our family."

The silence continued for a second longer, then there was a gasp. All the air in the room seemed to be drawn into lungs at once. Everyone turned to the Barneses. Now, how would they act? The boy, of course, ought to be jerked up. But what would the parents say to each other? How would they slide past it?

The answer was laughter. Frank Barnes threw back his head and roared. Young Buck was embarrassed by the attention he had drawn, but his face showed no fear. He would not be humiliated. He frowned and looked at his plate.

Mamie Barnes was the most astonishing of all. She waited for her husband to catch his breath, then she said, in the same tone of laughter: "Frank, I don't know what's up, but you've been bragging again!"

The women felt terribly let down. It was inconceivable that the matter should end there, but that was just where it was going to end, it seemed. They each looked long and hard at Mamie Barnes and could not make up their minds whether to forgive her or not. The men felt, well, Frank Barnes had a way with his woman. It certainly was neat.

When the visit ended, nobody had learned much about the newcomers. It was a disappointment.

Man's Work

▷ ▷ ▷   Young Charles, who had finished his first year in high school, was aware of the contest waging between his grandmother and his father. They had started right after school closed. It was like all family disputes—fought mostly under cover, with hint and innuendo the principal weapon, and the significant silence used both for attack and for defence.

On this afternoon of a June Sunday, Young Charles lay in the stifling orchard where he had gone to read *Ivanhoe* after the midday meal. He was not reading, however, for his reading mind had been smothered by his listening mind. His father and his grandmother were at each other again.

"Are you going to town, Charles?" his grandmother asked.

Even the boy in the orchard knew that the question was not asked innocently. The tone was not quite bitter, but it was hard; it was a challenge. "Just you dare pretend you don't know what I mean!" his grandmother was warning his father.

The group on the front porch, sequestered in a narrow ribbon of north side shade from a sun that always burned hotter on Sundays (there was time to take note of it), acted as if the boy in the orchard were at the end of the world. After all, though they struggled for his possession, it was a principle which was involved and which dignified their stubborn refusal to admit the reality of unadmired facts. Principle was what Young Charles balked at; words, he understood, and facts could be mastered, school required it; but principle was an invention of grown-ups designed to magnify trifles.

Of the three persons in the porch group, only two counted.

The boy's father Big Charles (as he was called) sat apart, with a farm magazine spread out on his lap. If he was pressed too hard he would return to his reading. It was an old trick with him. He was a brawny man, his heavy hands having the color and the lumpiness of the clay of his fields. He was exacting of the horses he worked, of the tools he used, of the newspapers he read, but those who worked with him said he was a fair sort.

The father's mother sat with arms folded over her flat breast, her shoulders unbowed, her eyes unwearied. At an age when most people leave their chairs in the sun less and less frequently, she had taken on the burden of a new household within the last six years and was still carrying it, at her own insistence. She was a fighter who would do justice to any cause. She made a pulse of her devotion, and it was also her breath, her pillow in slumber and her crowing cock; she chewed it with her food, and it was a sovereign digestant; nothing distracted her.

The third person of the group was Young Charles' mother. A helpless invalid (she suffered from an ailment which could not be discussed in his presence), she had yielded her place at the head of the household to the older woman. She took no interest in what went on around her. If she interposed her thin voice at all it was to make some mild observation on the appearance of the neglected flower beds in front of the house, or a comparison of the number of flies, this year and last.

The question "Are you going to town?" was a threat and a challenge, but Big Charles made no effort to meet it. "I don't see what I'd go for."

The grandmother frowned, irritated because she had to waste words explaining what was perfectly understood.

"Humph! You know your mind as well's another. If you're not going it's because you've decided to put Young Charles in the hayfield tomorrow."

Big Charles smiled lazily, satisfied that he could not be touched.

"Well, I had thought of getting him to help me. And he's willing, told me so the other day. It won't hurt him none. What did you think I'd pay a hired man with? If it was a horse I was borrowing I could give him hay. But a man wants money, and I ain't seen any money in a long while."

"You always borrow for harvest times. I ain't heard you say you can't get money when you want it."

Young Charles had heard his father complain before this that the women folks didn't understand about money; they would not believe him when he said he was tired of borrowing every year to the limit of his crop and casting up his accounts a little behind or at best on even terms, with nothing to show for twelve months of effort. Today he avoided the issue.

"I never heard yet that work was hurtful to a boy. It's what they need. It's what makes 'em grow. We've all got to learn to work, and the longer you put off breakin' a boy in to it the more chances you take with him. I don't know how many I've seen with my own eyes take it into their heads they was too good for the lot of ordinary folks. First they take to wearin' their good clothes for every day, then before long they want to spend their evenings in town and have a little pocket money besides. By that time they ain't worth a nickel a dozen, not to themselves or anyone else. A boy doesn't like to work by nature, but if you give in to him you're doin' him a real wrong, that you are. So I say it's best to get him used to it, and before long he's got enough spunk to get along himself.

"Young Charles won't be workin' real hard. With these hay boats we use nowadays that slide along like bob-sleds, it's no trick to load 'em—not like it was when I began hayin', when you had to pitch up to a rack settin' on wheels. That put a kink in your back. I recollect that I didn't get much fun out of it, but I guess it didn't hurt me none."

The words were spoken without heat, but in a tone that expressed the speaker's faith in the truthfulness of his utterance and the complete disbelief in anything that might be said against him.

"There might be two ways of looking at that." The old lady was more than visibly annoyed. "It ain't helped your looks none—you're bowed in the middle as if you was picking things off the ground all the time. It ain't helped your charity none neither, and you're determined to make folks, including your son, do everything you had to do. Well, you've had your way. No one's had an easy time around you and never will."

The thrust was one that should have struck home, but Big Charles sat immobile and his bronzed face was deceptive. The old lady regretted her words, words which she had rarely uttered, and while she went on talking with scarcely a pause, she was for a time distracted. Meantime, Big Charles' wife, the living proof of the charge that no one lived an easy life around him, sat impassively. She was not listening.

"I've heard enough in my time of men boasting that hail nor snow nor high water could keep 'em from doing what they had a mind to do—but I don't know as I admire 'em for it any more. If other women folks stopped admiring and told 'em it wasn't necessary, which it isn't, we'd probably all live different. I've heard your arguments about how a man has to work into outlandish hours of the night to make a decent living, but I tell you this, Charles, your back profits from what your belly doesn't get. And if folks would just stop listening to your bragging you wouldn't be long finding you didn't have to work owl's hours.

"Least of all, there's no need to start a boy off before he's properly into his first long pants. You're like them priests I despise so, ketching youngsters before they know any better and giving 'em the whole gospel. Boys have years when they'll sop up anything like sponges, and I'd a lot rather see them take in some just plain foolishness than make plow horses out of 'em right from the start. They'll learn how to work all right, when they find their eating depends on it."

Big Charles laughed his lazy laugh, jarring the somnolent air no more than would the low drone of a passing bumble bee.

"Well, I wish you'd felt that way when I was a boy."

"I didn't know enough," the answer came back briskly. "Besides, your father was as blind as most men. His notion about character was that a man had none unless he was ornery and willing to abuse himself and others too."

A period of silence followed which left a void in the stifling Sunday afternoon as unsettling as the cessation of some natural phenomenon. An unexpected halt in the dripping from eaves after a summer storm will produce a similar sensation of waiting, a kind of impalpable itching which no scratching can appease.

Young Charles lay in the heat soaked orchard, waiting for the resumption of the word patter. If it ever did continue he never knew, for he fell asleep, his unclenched hand fallen short of the Scott romance.

▽

"Wake up, boy!"

Looking up through a subdued light which he first took for the haze of drowsiness, but soon discovered to be due to the fading intensity of the setting sun, Young Charles saw his father standing above him.

"Wake up, boy! Cows won't come without a man goes after them. They won't milk themselves neither. No, nor crops won't get planted and post holes get dug, for all the women folks say."

Father and son grinned, the one showing that he prized willingness, the other because he lived on the tone of a voice.

▽

Walking down to the meadow, his sunburned blond head bobbing against the green of a fenced-in wheatfield, he tried to decide to which, his father or his grandmother, he felt closest. He could not tell. He might be the cause of the struggle, but he never knew for a whole day together on which side his interest lay. If his father asked him to help with the haying, as he had, the answer was that work must be a good thing, since his father expected him to share in it. On the other hand, when his grandmother looked at him with one of her sharp looks (she had sharp eyes for a granny, everybody remarked on it), and said "Boy, you don't look well. Your father shouldn't keep you in the sun so much," he felt that she must know what she was talking about and wondered if he were being treated badly. Not that he minded.

"What's the difference?" The problem ceased to interest him.

▽

On Monday morning he asked his grandmother to go down to the haymeadow after breakfast and watch him start off, but she only glared at Big Charles and said nothing.

When he came from the field for the midday meal an air of resignation had settled over the house, and his grandmother made no further gesture than to look at him critically, apparently to assure herself that he had had no arm or leg clipped off by the mowing sickle.

"Humph!" she croaked when Big Charles, thinking to calm any troubled out-of-sight waters, remarked:

"It beats me what a cracker-jack Charlie is on the mower. He didn't miss a spear of grass all morning."

Young Charles felt that he had entered a really new domain when, after lunch, his father led the way to the shady north side of the house. During haying and harvesting, from his earliest recollections, the hired men had always congregated there after the noon meal to smoke and swap stories and lie stretched out until one o'clock.

"Let's rest ourselves, Charlie," his father said, in the same neighborly tone he used with Elm Higgins when Elm came over to help for a few days. There were no peremptory commands of "Run in and fetch my tobacco!" or "Go down to the barn and see what the horses are fightin' about!" as in former days. He had done half-a-day's work and was entitled to a man's rest.

Indoors, Maria, the forty-year-old orphan, who had spent her entire life keeping house and cooking for about every family in the valley, was clattering the dishes about and shouting to the grandmother in the next room. She was saying:

"Men folks make it easy for themselves. Just don't you worry about Young Charles, Mrs. Durand. He'll get on to the tricks quick as the next one."

The house yielded no more than an uncertain internal rumble for an answer.

Young Charles smiled through his drowsiness. His grandmother's words seemed unreasonable, alien. After all, did she know what a boy wanted, what was good for him?

Any dislike of work which he might have felt, induced by his grandmother's arguments, had been dissipated by the morning's experience, when he had discovered that riding a mowing machine and cutting a full swath was both simple and pleasant. As he lay, relaxed, he was thinking that on the next occasion of a family dispute he would intervene and give his own view: "Work's nothing. A fellow does it and thinks nothing of it. It's like anything else. You just do it, and that's all." That would be his contribution, and then they would realize that all these weeks of bickering had been unnecessary.

The afternoon was not in every respect as pleasant as the morning had been. The sun was merciless, fifteen degrees hotter, he thought, and the nap in the shade after lunch had been seductive to one so recently arrived at man's estate. He had watched his father and the hired men get up after a leisurely half-hour, stretch themselves, and submit their necks to the yoke of their necessity as placidly as the horses being put into the traces; but when it came his turn he could not relish the part.

Early in the afternoon he overtook his father, who had stopped to tinker with his machine.

"I hit a stick of wood back there a piece and bent a sickle guard." His father spoke without lifting his head.

When the repair was made, Big Charles straightened himself, smiled reflectively, as if the sight of his son recalled some pleasant thought.

"Well, it's not so bad, hey, Charlie!" his father exclaimed, as he patted the flanks of the near horse.

"Oh, I like it!" Young Charles responded, and his voice was neither perfunctory, nor resigned, nor sad.

Big Charles chuckled and went back to his machine.

▽

Towards three-thirty in the afternoon, at a time when Charles was wholly absorbed in his man's vocation, his grandmother donned her huge sunbonnet and accompanied Maria to the field with a bucket of iced lemonade and a cloth covered plate of oatmeal cookies. Whether she had bowed to the inevitable and was coming with good will, or whether she was bent on carrying the battle to her adversary, she very likely did not know herself: opportunity would tell. Outwardly, she was complying with a tradition of the women folks in bringing to the men this reminder of rest that should come after labor, of community of thought and effort.

She had not advanced far down the field with the chattering Maria when a light rumble of flying hooves caused both women to glance to the rear. In dismay, they beheld a sorrel colt, his coat spangling in the sun, come dashing up, crash to a halt when fifty paces away, then toss his head and go off with a rush in a skirting movement. His curly tail dipped a salute, and in a moment he was out of gunshot.

"Maria!" Mrs. Durand cried. "We forgot to close the gate!"

A later thought caused her to look aghast towards the flying colt.

"Give me that lemonade. And Maria, run as fast as your legs will carry you to Young Charles. He's driving the colt's mother. Hurry! Run! Stop those machines!"

Maria was off with "Oh, dear me!" her chubby legs jarring her breath out in gasps.

$\triangledown$

Young Charles never knew how it had happened. He might have been wandering through interplanetary space, attuned to the clicking of the sickle of infinity.

The disaster was heralded. In its flight toward him it halted at the crest of a rise, some distance away, like a sun spangle caught for a moment on a crest of water. He might have watched it race towards him, again like a sun spangle, hurled from a mirror across space. And the sudden, shrill whinny of Susan, the strapping sorrel mare on the off side, next to the sickle bar, should have sounded as a trumpet in his ears.

The concluding action was swift and direct.

Charles looked up, after the second whinny of the mare, and at the same instant he saw the colt dash into the uncut alfalfa meadow some yards ahead of the team. The mowing machine at that time was still going forward, of its own volition, it might have seemed, since no one was willing its motion.

The picture of Bucky, the colt, prancing forward with erect head and elastic movement, was not complete in Charles' mind. When he tried to see it "as it was," he found that instead of unfolding the steps in sequence his memory went backward to recreate over and over his first impression of the colt advancing, his golden coat gleaming, his hooves stamping at the earth.

The reason for this uncertainty was that at the critical moment

Charles ceased to look. His eyes blinked, as if a splinter had come flying past his head. Perhaps his mind blinked. He did not faint, though that was what was thought afterward; he simply fell from the machine, and in falling gave that slight tug upon the reins which was all that was necessary to halt the team.

Then he heard floundering, and knew that Bucky was trying to stand upright. But he did not look. He knew what was happening, and that he should do something, but movement was impossible. He lay where he had fallen.

"Wake up, boy!"

The call, as familiar as the dawn, sounded now with an accent of scorn he thought.

His father stood miles above him, the moving muscles of his strained face only dimly discernible. In a moment so chaotic Young Charles still remembered everything that had been in his mind these past few days, but he felt that a mistake had been made. It was only now that he understood what his father and grandmother had been arguing about—it was about *work*. Now he understood that word. And now, though he recognized his father well enough, and knew that a response was expected of him, he did not smile his willingness.

"Wake up! Why didn't you stop the team?" His father must have shouted a dozen times, perhaps with an infuriating realization of the senselessness of the question.

"I didn't see him in time," Young Charles answered weakly, and suddenly caught a glimpse of blood spurting and turning black upon the green alfalfa leaves.

At that point his mind really did go blank. An instant later, or so it seemed, his grandmother was holding his hand and clucking in her comforting way.

As soon as he felt her presence, he surprised even himself by drawing away. It was most unexpected, but it could not have been otherwise. This clucking, this hand patting was not what he wanted. No. The way it was at that moment, father and grandmother were equally strange to him.

Young Charles left the farm soon after that, not for the sake of spending his evenings in town and dressing in his best clothes, but to go to work in a drugstore. After all that talk, all that argumentation, he was answering the question himself and he didn't care whether his answer pleased anybody or not. But he didn't say that. There was no violent quarrel, although there was unspoken bitterness of which everyone tasted.

Big Charles let his son go his own way, because after what had happened he did not care to keep him. "He may straighten up in a few years. But if he don't, he's a no-[accounter] right now." That was the conclusion of Big Charles, who was an exacting man.

The grandmother was perhaps the most worried of all. She considered herself responsible for the boy's decision, and she wasn't sure that she ought to have encouraged him to take a different view about work than his father held. She was saddened by the breach.

"Folks ought to be careful of speaking," she said to Maria, the cook. "It ain't enough to mean what you say—you want to be sure you can bear to see your words acted on."

Going to School

▷ ▷ ▷   Dawn had come but it was still dark. The lights from the houses shone almost as brightly as they would have in the middle of night. A stiff wind came up at intervals and the sky over the eastern mountains was unmistakably growing lighter every minute. Roosters were crowing and occasionally a door opened and a man came out to spit and look at the sky.

A young boy stood by the dirt road and peered toward the fringe of timber that lay a quarter of a mile eastward from the town. He could see or hear nothing and was munching on an apple. In one hand he carried a lunch bucket.

Suddenly he heard horses snorting and blowing in the cold air. And then he could hear buggy wheels rattling over the frozen ground. He finished his apple in several large bites and tossed the core aside. He wiped his mouth with the sleeve of his coat and put his mitten on the hand that had held the apple. A moment later a team of horses and a buggy materialized out of the mist and gloom and a voice called out sharply:

"Whoa, there, cayuses!"

A girl's voice followed immediately after: "Good morning, Joey! Are we late?"

"Naw, you're not late. I just came from the house." He put his lunch pail in the back of the rig and climbed onto the seat.

"Put these blankets around you good. It's terribly cold." The girl helped to wrap the blankets around his legs.

"That's good enough," he said before she had finished.

The scraggy team of mares was put at a trot and the buggy was on its way again. It was precarious footing, however, and though they picked their feet up quickly and made a motion of trotting they couldn't manage anything better than a fast walk.

The sky had turned a shade lighter and the town could be made out more distinctly. It was a forlorn place clinging to the edge of the timber. Not a house was painted; they were all shanties.

On the left the mountains were still black and heavy mist hid their wide bases. High up among the peaks a ray of light gleamed now and then on a snow bank. Off to the right was the rolling prairie land and clumps of trees could be seen along some creek banks. There was a mist over the prairie, too, and it seemed dull and dead out that way. A chill breeze cut into the faces of the three travelers in the buggy and made them keep their heads pulled low on their shoulders.

Gene, the driver, was a thin-faced youth whose eyes watered constantly in the cold wind. His jaws stood out rigidly and his skin was smooth, for he hadn't yet put a razor to his face. He didn't talk as much as the others; he sat and brooded and wore a long face.

Ada sat in the middle and her blue eyes were always twinkling. She had a clear, healthy complexion and the stinging wind made her cheeks glow warmly. She was eighteen at most, yet she looked older.

Joe, who had waited at the roadside, knew of nothing better in the world than to be sitting where he was, beside Ada. The buggy seat was narrow and he was pressed closely against her; he could feel her warmth up and down his right side. Joe was younger than the others, four years younger than Ada, but he never thought of that.

When they came to the bridge at the end of the first mile the team slowed down and looked cautiously from one side to the other as they went up the approach. The bridge planks were white with frost and after the buggy had passed over, two neat tracks were left behind. When the bridge was crossed, the horses picked up their shambling trot again. The breath came out of their nostrils in white clouds and formed a coating of frost on the hair of their necks. They were an unkempt team of little mares with their long winter's hair; bits of straw and their night's bedding still clung to their sides. Gene forgot to curry them most of the time.

A serious conversation was being carried on in the buggy. Joe had said: "My folks had a fight last night and we may be moving away one of these days."

"No! You don't mean right away—before school is out?" Ada asked.

"Well, no, not that soon."

"What was they fighting about?" Gene asked.

"Why, ma thinks that we made a bad move when we bought lots during the boom. She says we might as well have thrown the money in the river. But pa laughs about it. 'Money's no good if you don't use it,' he says. 'You just as well take a gambling chance once in a while; all you have is a gambling chance; and even then you're bound to lose,' he says."

"Were they angry?" Ada wanted to know.

"Oh yes, I suppose all the neighbors heard them."

"Well," Gene said, "your ma's right. Nobody's going to make any money out of that town!"

"You don't know anything about it! You've heard dad say that," his sister reminded him.

"We could have made a little money last fall. We were offered three hundred dollars more for the shop than it cost us. But ma said it wasn't enough. She got mad last night when we reminded her of it."

Gene went off on a tangent.

"Your folks don't fight any more than ours," he said. "There's a wrangle at home every day."

"We have dad to thank for that. If it was mother alone it would be different."

But Gene couldn't agree with that.

"It takes two to make a quarrel and she nags as much as he does. She doesn't do it outright, that's the difference. She goes around complaining until somebody has to get mad."

"She has something to complain about, I think! Not one of you kids ever help her and she's had ten of us to take care of."

"Well," said Gene, "I'll tell you one thing, Joe, don't get married! A poor man's got to work his fingers to the bone as it is, but if he gets married, he's sunk!"

But Joe disagreed. No. It wasn't that bad! It depended on yourself—and, of course, on whom you married.

"Do you think married people are never happy? Sure, lots of them are! But you've got to be in love. I don't think my folks were ever in love; they don't act like it, and that's why they row."

"You talk like a calf! What's love? I ain't seen any yet," Gene said.

What, no love! And Joe sat there burning with it! He knew no unhappiness. It was true that his father and mother made things unpleasant with their misunderstandings and uncharitable accusations. His sister was half an idiot and sat at home laughing and crying by turns and trying to draw pictures on the windowpane with her pencil. There was no money in the home most of the time though his father ran a butcher shop.

Joe lived in the midst of many things that might have been thought unpleasant, yet he went through them unscathed. When he sat beside Ada he was content. He thought of finer things; it might even be imagined that he saw them dancing by like the fence posts on either side that went flying past in an endless chain. For seven months, ever since school opened in September, he had been riding with the Silverthorns, and ever since Christmas when Ada kissed him at the School Entertainment he had been engulfed in a great world of mist and warm dew.

The sun had burst over the mountains and the gloom that had lurked in the hollows and over against the timber all disappeared. The few scattered banks of snow that lay in the nearby fields sparkled and looked whiter. The frost disappeared from the horses' necks and they got over the road with a freer gait.

On and on the road led in a straight line down the valley. The mountains were always parallel and as one traveled along one could see ever new angles to the peaks and canyons.

Gene sat on the driver's side in his peculiar hunched over fashion and he held the lines with listless hands. He hissed at the horses and cursed them soundly when they slowed to catch a breath or when one of them slipped on a patch of ice. He seemed to dream, perhaps of the dreary round of chores that awaited him when he returned at night, perhaps of his father with his savage temper, or perhaps he dreamed of freedom from these things.

Ada, as she sat there, wore a half smile and an eager expression as if she expected every moment to come upon some marvellous discovery. No one could think of calling her a girl, exactly; she held her head with the studied grace of a woman; in a few years she would be a little too fleshy and then she would be a woman indeed.

For Joe there could be no accounting for her charm. He never relaxed in the seat beside her; he was in a continual flux of emotions. Something happened almost every day that brought him more deeply under her spell. It wasn't much, a mere nothing, but he came to regard each new day with wistful expectation. Anything might happen! In these past few months he had suddenly begun to feel like a matured young man. He looked backward from the pinnacle of his fourteen years and he saw his childhood lying somewhere in the indeterminate past.

The conversation had gone to other things.

"I've made up my mind to study law when I get to college," Joe said.

"Do you really plan to go to college, then?" Ada asked him.

"Yes. Ma always wanted me to be a lawyer. When she got her divorce they made her say a lot of things that weren't true but she couldn't help herself. So she's always wanted me to study law and make up for it, though I don't see what can be done now."

"That will be fine! When I come to get my divorce I'll see you the first thing. I'll say: 'Joey, my husband's mean to me. Please get me a divorce right away!' And then what will you do?"

Joe's tongue failed him and he couldn't think of a witty reply. He said: "I'll go and kick the seat of his pants up between his shoulders!"

Ada was surprised and didn't know whether to laugh or not, but Gene roared aloud and the horses threw up their heads and trotted faster.

Now they were approaching town. The seven mile ride was ending. The sun was an hour above the mountains and the frostiness had almost gone from the air. The sky was completely free from cloud and mist and a golden effulgence poured down upon the land.

The school was the first building on the left as they entered town. It stood by itself in the center of a large yard. There were tall poles standing upright with cross bars over the top, these were the swings where the children played.

The school building was long and narrow and built in two stories. The lower half was covered with shingles and painted brown; white clapboards covered the upper half. From all directions one could see pupils coming towards the school in vehicles of all descriptions—some were on horseback, some had single horse rigs, while others drove a team; and now a green and white school-wagon came lumbering down the lane.

When Gene stopped his team of brown mares before the entrance gate, there were fully a half-hundred youngsters jumping around; they laughed and shouted and banged one another with their dinner pails. Something as fluid as electricity and as startling took possession of the three in the buggy. They looked at each other, at the crowd of pupils, and began to laugh. This was school! There was nothing else like it!

Joe got down and helped Ada from the buggy; then he drove with Gene to the stable to unhitch the horses.

It was a strange business, this going to school. Out at home things went their humdrum way; the father would be stamping around the fields to see how near the frost was to leaving the ground or he would be in the granary fanning his seed wheat; the mother would be in the kitchen mixing her bread or else out in the yard feeding the chickens. But in school it was different; they read about the capital of one State and the area of another; they learned about Nigeria and Liberia and Abyssinia and Lake Titicaca high in the mountains; they used words like "hypotenuse" and "congruent" in geometry; they found out that there had been a French Revolution and a War of the Spanish Succession and that Shakespeare had written many plays and was no doubt the greatest man in the world. But when they went home they kept their discoveries under their hats. It would never do to let the old folks feel that they didn't know everything; they would have only one way to answer such a charge, and that was with the stick.

Joe knew well enough how it was. He sat in his classroom and swallowed everything greedily. His head was full of things that had happened thousands of miles away and hundreds of years ago. But he knew better than to talk about them when he got home. There was no sense in being laughed at.

"Wipe your nose!" his father would say if Joe should tell him that Rome had been a great Empire ruled over by Julius Caesar who talked Latin.

The morning's ride had been a pleasant event in its way, and the school hours were themselves filled with moments of ecstasy; but the pleasantest time of all was when they drove home at night.

The air was warm then, so warm that coats were left unbuttoned and one could crane one's neck around and have a look at the scenery; and there were heavy shadows lying across the land. At the big cattle ranch along the foothills it was feeding time and the steers could be heard blowing and bellowing. The feeding wouldn't last much longer; soon there would be a coating of green over the hills and prairie and the stockman could leave off measuring his haystacks with his eye.

But there was no green grass yet. Indeed, the frost had by no means left the ground. The first few inches were free and soft with mud but down below there was something hard. And when morning came around everything would be stiff with frost again.

Everyone felt the glory of those first spring afternoons. Even Gene's shabby mares held their heads with a certain pride and they took to the long road with renewed energy as they swung around the corner and left the school house behind. And Gene himself was not the same. Whatever sparkle of humor his system could muster then came to the surface and played about for a moment like faint blue lightning on the horizon. But he wasn't at home when it came to playing with wit; he would stumble around for a while and before long take to cursing something or other as a more effective way of getting over what he wanted to say. No, Gene didn't fit into this world of youthful thoughts and feelings. He had shrivelled already. He had been broken to the plow when he was too young a colt and now he could never enjoy running wild.

Ada was touched by the same searing process. If she escaped at all it was something to marvel at. She was the eldest in the family of ten and she had borne the brunt of it all; she had mothered nine of the ten children; but it hadn't proved too heavy a task for her. She was charming and sprightly for an elderly woman of eighteen!

The family of ten was gradually becoming valuable as time went on. Over half of them were working now and if the first ones had been put at it a little too early it was easier for the late comers.

Ada had kissed Joe at Christmas time and here it was March and he hadn't awakened from the spell yet! He hadn't enjoyed it at the time, it is true. He had been too ashamed and confused to know just what had happened. Besides, the room had been full of people. Since then the event had revealed its proper significance. He would know how to act the next time.

His father and mother spent all their time making life unpleasant for each other. Every night when Joe came home they were at it. He lived his life on the road to school; the night was only spent in waiting for another day. Sometimes he couldn't avoid being drawn into a family melee; he went about looking so dreamy and absent-minded that his parents must turn and attack him occasionally. And he became more pointedly aware of the two worlds he was attempting to straddle. But on the road to school much was left behind and he dreamed astounding dreams. In fact, it would be hard to say which of Joe's thoughts were real and which were but the froth and mist of some dream pot bubbling over. And on this very day one dream, at least, was to put on a cloak of reality and meet Joe face to face.

For over seven months the two brown mares had performed their task in the most irreproachable manner possible. They had trotted mile after mile without complaint—though it is true that a fast-legged man could have kept abreast of them at any time; and as they went they looked neither on one side nor the other but with bowed heads kept the middle of the road. Viewing them critically, they were commonplace and shabby and a whip lash falling on their scrawny backs brought no protest. Yet on this day they did a most unexpected and unreasonable thing.

They had been trotting along with their eyes glued to the road and the three young people in the buggy behind them had been engaged in a methodical discussion of the day's events. The mares were shedding heavily and it was really difficult to talk as one had to stop at every other word and spit out a horse hair. Gene sat with the lines held loosely in his hands and he seemed to be pondering things in his uninspired way.

And then three pigs appeared suddenly.

They had escaped their pen and were in the lane, looking for the feast of green grass they had scented on the wind, no doubt. They had been hidden from view behind a pile of last year's tumble weeds and just as the buggy came abreast of them they ran into the road to sniff the air and decide which way to run. They grunted and squealed and one old sow grew confused and tried to run between the legs of Tricksey, the mare on the rear side.

Tricksey was patient enough but she couldn't be expected to allow a pig to run between her legs. She sat back on her haunches for just a second and then she shot ahead like a cannon ball and it was a wonder that the tug straps didn't snap like cotton twine. Tricksey's mate caught the panic too and it took only a moment to get their legs and harness untangled and then they were off!

The buggy swayed from side to side; it dashed into the gutter and balanced for a moment on two wheels, then it straightened itself and lurched to the other side of the road. All the loose bolts and rods and wheel spokes were rattling as they never had rattled before.

It was strange to see what happened inside the buggy. At the first unexpected move Gene straightened himself in the seat. When the horses took the bits into their teeth and began their mad gallop straight for destruction—he lost no time in contemplation. With one movement he thrust the lines into Ada's hands and with a second motion he had vaulted out of the buggy and clear of the wheels. He landed in a lump on the roadside.

Joe sat there in a daze. If he had tried to talk he would have stuttered. The buggy swayed perilously, the slightest obstruction sent the wheels bounding into the air. He probably would have continued to sit in a trance until they had smashed against a fence or telephone post if he hadn't thrown his hand out involuntarily to balance himself. In doing so he grasped the lines. The next moment he had braced his feet against the dashboard and was pulling for all he was worth. He was thoroughly frightened by now and he had the strength of desperation.

Joe stopped the mares by running them into a sand bank at the corner of the lane where the road had been cut through a low hill. The moment they stopped he scrambled out and took them by the bridles. He was trembling. He led them around into the road again before they tried to climb the hill. He kept saying over and over:

"You damn mutts! You damn mutts! Hold up now!"

Gene didn't overtake them for half an hour. He came up the road with a limp in one leg.

Ada looked at him with amazement and contempt. "Why on earth did you jump?" she asked.

He didn't answer until he had examined the buggy and harness to see that nothing was broken. He climbed wearily onto the seat and he looked like quite an old man.

"Why did I jump? What do you suppose! Am I going to risk my neck for a team of scrub cayuses? Not much! I'll die soon enough as it is!"

Ada scorned such premature wisdom. "Look at little Joe!" she said. "He isn't thinking of himself all the time! He acts like a little man!— Why Joe!" She turned to him ecstatically. "You're so brave!"

With a swift movement she grasped his coat and pulled him close and kissed him, once on the cheek and once on the mouth. Then she laughed gently and let him go.

Joe had anticipated her action. He had braced himself to meet it— to no avail. His courage gave way and he turned red; after the second kiss he actually put up his hands to protect himself! And immediately afterwards he felt miserable. He pushed his shoulders up and drew in his head to hide his confusion.

"You girls make me sick!" Gene said, "always kissing people!"

"We don't kiss everybody, do we, Joe?"

What could Joe say!

They started down the road again. The mares had spent themselves and were content to go at an ordinary pace though they threw their heads from side to side and blew through their nostrils with the pride of their deed.

Darkness was coming now and there was coolness in the air. After the buggy had disappeared in the shadows and mist that arose from the cooling earth, the wheels could still be heard rattling over the graveled road. One more day of school was ending.

▷ ▷ ▷ THE CITY

Manhattan Wedlock

▷ ▷ ▷   Felix and Margot weren't living together at the moment. Their friends, knowing about it, were getting what laughs they could out of the situation—a privilege of friends.

"They won't get over this for a while. In fact, it may break them up."

Margot's tenderhearted brother, Ted, was telling me the story in a Forty-Second Street cafe, which, if it wasn't the world's noisiest enclosure between four walls, was at least no place to hear a fire engine siren.

Ted was one of those vultures, one of those forty-year-old bachelors who smell disaster in every marriage, who get their claws into the situation early, and who have a special cackle to celebrate the final rending apart.

He was a lawyer, partly bald, moderately successful in real estate practice, and always full of gossip and at least half-full of rye and soda. His practice was a mystery, since a large part of his time was spent in meeting places of one sort or another. The answer to the mystery, one learned in time, was a grinding, tireless partner who did all the paper work while Ted legged it about and bagged the clients.

On this day, mid-week, a sudden downpour of summer rain had driven me to cover in that clang-bang Forty-Second Street beer shop, and the first person I recognized was Ted, half-drenched, looking for a table, and brushing water drops from his clothes with something of the angry disdain of a wet cat. Seeing me, his face brightened, as it did every time he met me of late. He knew, you see, that I was seriously in love and it gave him devilish pleasure to insinuate asininity in my behavior. As it happened, we knew a lot of people in common and there wasn't much I could do to avoid him. I was forever meeting him and listening to one of his tiresome stories about plundered wedlock. He collected them especially for my benefit. I alternated between ignoring him and threatening him with murder.

I didn't like Ted, as perhaps I have suggested. I was really in love.

I knew Felix and Margot very well—in fact, admired them. Felix, tall and blond and full of laughter; Margot, quick, darkly beautiful, impulsive and racy. They fought with a kind of merry earnestness which made their scraps community fun. Usually there was a love feast, to which the friends were invited and given all the details. And sometimes the fighting started on a new cycle right there, because they couldn't agree on how the fight started, how it reached its climax, or who gave in first.

"By the way . . ." Ted gave me a searching look out of his greenish eyes, his pointed moustache stiffening as his lips tightened, "have you noticed that their quarrels get sharper all the time, and take longer to patch up? You haven't noticed it? Perhaps you wouldn't. It's a gift, noticing people."

His dapper insolence ruffled me a bit. "In your case, I often wonder how much is observation and how much dyspepsia. Do you take bicarbonate?"

He smiled it away. One couldn't get him angry. That was the hell of it. Sometimes he would look hurt if you pressed him, but no more.

"It's a family trait, this gift of observing. Now, Margot has it to a degree amounting almost to genius. She can put her finger on a person's get-up ten seconds after meeting him, if he has any character to work on."

"Yes, yes. I know Margot. But why is this last scrape any different from any of the others? And what makes you so sure it isn't going to be patched up in short order?"

"Well . . ." he settled himself back in his chair, his fingers curling

around the damp highball glass. Of all life's pleasures, the greatest for
him, I believe, was settling back like that with a good story of a
bankrupt marriage to spill. He knew how to bring out all the petti-
ness, all the miserable little inconsequences which snag the feet of
people in love. It wasn't decent.

"Well, it must have been something, this row of theirs. They
surpassed themselves. You know how Margot is—quick as a flash,
intuitive, always in motion, jolly. . . . Well, she's my sister and I
shouldn't brag about her, but she's quite a bunch—all warmth and
affection. . . ."

"O.K. O.K. Spill it."

"Oh, this can't be rushed. Margot has to be done quite properly.
Before she met Felix she was making a good thing out of her writing.
Not everybody remembers that. They think of them as a team, and
that it was Felix got her started. But that's screwy. She was writing
good stuff—woman's page stuff—some kind of column—I never read
it—but she was top-notch. Waiter! Rye and soda! Two!

"What Felix did was get her into the theater. And a good thing, I
agree. He had, was it two plays before he met her? Not successes—
but corking writing—forget what they were called."

I knew all that, knew the plays.

"Never mind . . . I'm trying to get the picture of this thing in mind.
There they were—both making a good thing in their own rights.
Both young—having lots of fun. Then they decided to get married—
what was to be gained? Margot says the first time she met him at
somebody's party she knew she was going to marry him—inside of
half a minute after meeting him she knew it. I can't understand what
kept her from telling him on the spot—that's her style—always
talking out of turn. I agree with Felix about that part of it."

Somewhere, an aluminum tray full of tin dishes got loose at the top
of a half-mile flight of stone steps and banged in multiple metallic
discords all the way to the bottom. We shuddered.

"I'd like this place," Ted remarked, "if the crickets didn't keep me
awake. Let's see—did I get them married yet? Oh, yes. It was while
they were getting married. Margot, the fool, wanted it done in a
church. So we were all over there—is it Epiphany? or Trinity? I
wouldn't remember. It was a rehearsal—yes, we were having a re-

hearsal. She and Felix went up the aisle—oh, yes, it's coming back. I marched her up the aisle. I was giving her away, it seems. And finally we got them standing there together before the Reverend School-craft—dear old man. He was tall and slow and lean headed—and he wore glasses. I don't know why I should remember that—but I remember perfectly what Margot did. The music had just squeaked out—kind of raggedy—like a real rehearsal. We were all in our places—seeing how it was going to be—everybody wanting a drink. Then Margot smiled that sweet smile she has.

" 'Dr. Schoolcraft,' she piped up, 'You're a tired man. You've been taking care of people at intimate moments like marrying and chris-tening and burying for so long you're kind of bored by it. I see all at once how people expect a lot of you at such times, and how thankless they are for the swell show you put on. You need something to bring back your springiness. A young wife would do it, but you're the kind of old dear who'll be around for your own golden wedding day. Maybe the best thing for you would be a new hobby, something that would start you over all fresh. How about stamps, Doctor? Have you ever collected them? Or coins, maybe?'

"There was much more—that's all I remember. Everybody was in stitches—except for the aristocratic Dr. Schoolcraft—and Felix. Felix was kind of paralyzed—thought she'd gone off her nut. What I mean is—that was his first moment of doubt. It happens to everybody at some point—and then the damage's done. That doubt, just a pinprick maybe, is the seat of infection. People forget all about it—go about the business of being married—sometimes for years—but not always. The poison's at work, and sooner or later the lesion becomes visible. They try to save themselves, if they're decent meaning peo-ple—and we most are—by cutting away at the infected part. Patch and make up, they call it. It doesn't help. The virus spreads, breaks out in a new place, another cutting is required. The wound never heals. . . ."

"For Christ's sake," I barked. "That glass has been empty for ten minutes. Get it filled and change your figure of speech. Waiter!"

He looked mildly surprised and reproachful. "You're so sensitive about a small matter. You don't trust my observations, so why should it get under your skin?"

"You were getting anesthetized—talking in a stupor. I want you to get on with the story."

He shrugged. "That is one of Margot's deepest traits. I could have told him—but naturally he wouldn't have listened—or he would have thought that because he loved her she would change anything he didn't like. Love is like that. A mere brother hasn't a chance. Margot, you know, is proud of her mind—and she has a right to be. She always beat the rest of the kids to the punch when it came to spelling and figuring problems and making speeches. At Wellesley she went in for everything, and came home plastered with trophies, like a channel swimmer. Plastered, besides. I met her at Grand Central and had to take her home and put her to bed. I think it was Wellesley."

"Was it Grand Central?" I asked, trying to catch him off guard. "And before you switch back to telling about your daddy and mama and granddaddy and grandmammy, remember that I'm still waiting to hear why you think this last spat has finished them off. I'm skeptical."

He took his own time. "Felix got her into playwrighting. He's no slouch at sizing up people himself, and he discovered that she had a knack for dialogue—not a knack, a damn good talent. Those two plays they've done together are as clever as anything that's hit Broadway since the Dutch kept their cows downtown. Or do I exaggerate?"

"Maybe slightly."

"Well, maybe slightly. I'm trying to get the whole picture, if you'll stop interrupting every two minutes—practically every two words. And why don't you order something to drink while I get started again!

"You've been at parties with them when Margot would be standing drinking a cocktail with someone, a perfect stranger, maybe their principal guest—and she'd start undressing him in public. And everybody'd think it was a swell game—all but the guest—and Felix. The guest would go home red in the face and frothing, and Felix would light into Margot. She was killing off all his friends. One night after a scene like that the fellow phoned Felix after the party and asked who was that bitch he was talking to. Imagine that!

"I don't know whether the word got to you, but a couple of weeks ago Felix heard of this Wall Street broker who was moving up-town. . . ."

I'd heard all about Hadley Smith—who hadn't? He'd cleaned up in the Curb Market, the story ran, and had a hankering for the theater. As a boy milking cows out in Iowa, he'd seen a roadshow at the local Opera House one night, and the leading lady had given him a permanent fit of nostalgia. That was the way the newspaper boys wrote it up. And now, flea circuses, midgets (Mr. Morgan's midget), bearded women—they'd all heard about him and were trying to get into his uptown hideaway. The crush was terrific. Fresh money was that scarce.

"You know, then," Ted took the bone between his teeth once more, "that Smith has owned the Puck Theater for about a year and already has several plays scheduled for this fall? Then I can shorten the tale. Why don't you order something to drink for a change?"

"To shorten the tale, here are Felix and Margot with their swell new play, and nobody with money enough to book passage on the Staten Island ferry to visit a dying mother. Felix hears of this Smith fellow and managed—he won't say how. . . ."

I couldn't hold out any longer. It had to end. The rye was beginning to make my mind wander and if he didn't come to the point at once we'd both forget what it was about.

"Let me tell it. I haven't talked to Felix, but I know what you're going to say. They get an appointment with the secretive Mr. Smith and start to tell him about the play, see? Then in the middle of it Margot breaks up the show by telling the man's fortune. So what?"

"But it's all in what she told him, you brute! Besides, that's not the finale. It's in what Felix said to her afterward. . . ."

A heavy hand hit me a wallop on the back and I all but skinned my chin on the table. It was Felix, looking like the ghost of an unwashed soul.

Felix was a tall boy, tall and blond. He had the shiniest and waviest hair outside of California. Ordinarily he looked pink-cheeked and hearty. His laughter drew people around him as easily as would a man pulling rabbits out of a traffic cop's pants pocket on Forty-Second Street. But today, his sails flapped. He had not been eating or sleeping enough and had been drinking too much. His mouth sagged tiredly.

He sat down on my side of the wall booth and signalled the waiter, but not to order a drink.

"Bernard . . ." that was the waiter's name—"if a call comes for me, I'm here, understand?"

We had no further business for the waiter at the moment, so he went away.

Felix added: "I'm not giving her a chance to say she called and couldn't get me. I let everybody know where I am and where I'm going next. And what do you think? She hasn't called me in a week!"

I had a bright idea. "She's waiting for you to call. Why don't you try it? After all . . ."

"I've tried. The maid says she's out."

"Oh!"

"You see, Felix," Ted helpfully explained, "this has gone deeper than you realize. If I were you, I'd get out of town for a while."

"Aw, shut up!"

At that, we all sat glumly for a minute, until it occurred to me that we needed something to drink. When I asked Felix what he wanted, he didn't hear me. I ordered black coffee for him.

"It would have been all right if I hadn't said what I did to her. That was what hurt."

I happened to glance at Ted and found him practically beaming. He raised his eyebrows at me in a way that made me want to strangle him.

"Ted has been sympathizing with you," I commented.

"Sympathizing? Oh, yeh. So I imagine." Felix couldn't get sidetracked. His mind operated like a steamshovel—going down for its load, coming up to disgorge, going down, coming up, going down. . . .

"There we were, in this guy's office. We had just started. You know how it is at first. You don't say much. You're lighting cigarettes, getting settled in chairs. Did I tell you about his office? No? It's tremendous—immense—I mean it's really large. Like Grand Central concourse. And there's this guy Smith off in one corner at a shiny desk. And he's got ship models everywhere, and tiger rugs, and floor lamps, and sofas so big you think you're alone on a desert island when you sit on one. We crowded around as close as we could to his desk, but as it was, we were practically shouting across Forty-Second Street to one another.

"He made some crack about being stifled for years. His downtown office had been cramped, I gathered. So when he moved uptown he really got himself some space. Had all the partitions knocked down. He was spreading himself.

"So I thought it sounded like a good idea, and so did Margot—and then she opened up on him. He had pulled the trigger and she was off.

" 'Mr. Smith, I see how it is. This is your rebirth. You've cracked some kind of a shell, and here you are. You feel swell, don't you? I can see it in your face. You're like a boy turned loose in a candy store. But there is more than that. You're a man that's been afraid. You haven't dared do the things you wanted to do until you could make it safe. That's why you stuck to the broker's business. It was easy for you, but it wasn't what you wanted. To you, it was dull business, no allure. You were saving your excitement for the last, when you couldn't get burned. And now, you're going to pay for your prudence. The theater will be flat and dreary. Because it won't be what you've been waiting for. If you had started to produce plays when you were young and short of money, then you'd have had plenty of excitement. But this way, all you have to do is buy what you want—plays, actors, managers, designers—the works. Is that fun? No. It's no good playing it safe. But I'll tell you what you can do. . . .'

"She had the man on the ropes, gasping. She'd met him only two minutes before. We'd just got seated.

" 'I'll tell you what you can do. . . .' she says. 'Get yourself a dizzy blond. You're not married, anyhow. Get yourself the dizziest one you can find and let her throw a real scare into you. If you stick it out without running away, then maybe there's hope. . . .' "

Felix groaned at that point. "That's as far as we got. Smith flagged her down. 'Thanks for the swell advice,' he says to her. 'I have another appointment in two minutes. Will you two tell me in about half a dozen words what you want of me?' You could hear ice cubes rattling in his mouth. Margot said it was bum bridgework. Anyhow . . .

"We didn't have a chance, because up to then we hadn't said a word about the play, and you can't talk about a play with a stopwatch on you. I didn't even try. Just asked if we could see him again. He wouldn't budge an inch. Said to call him up. I'd already spent a week getting that appointment.

"So there we were, standing outside his door, and Margot trying to make me laugh it off. . . ."

Ted opened his mouth to make a noise like a fiend, but caught me glaring at him and subsided.

Felix was still tranced. "She didn't mind my calling her dumb and wooden-headed—it was what I finally said, when we got back to the apartment—just before she threw the broom down the stairwell at me. . . ."

I saw Bernard the waiter in the distance, dodging between loaded trays and barging toward us as rapidly as his fallen arches would permit. Something had hurried him, and it wasn't a customer.

He came up to our table like a spent marathon runner. He lunged at Felix. "Mr. Cavendish. On the telephone. Quick. They said you should hurry."

Felix looked up without catching the idea. He had been on the point of telling me what he had said to Margot.

I nudged him. "Telephone."

"Oh, telephone!" He practically threw the table over on Ted's lap. "Hold the wire!"

Bernard attempted to run interference, but one sweep of Felix' long arm disposed of him. After that, it was a swell bit of open field running.

Ted sighed resignedly. "He thinks it'll be Margot."

"Two to one it is Margot!" I flared up at his persistent cynicism. Actually, I didn't think it would be, but I was getting unreasonable.

I wasn't right, and I wasn't wrong, though we didn't get the facts until we were in a cab bucking the Broadway flood on a rainy afternoon. Felix had bolted out of the phone booth almost at once, without coming near us had waved toward the door. It was a scramble to get away from the table and get the check paid before he disappeared.

"Eleanor the maid called. Said Margot's been sick for two days. Eleanor called on her own hook. Imagine. And she's feverish. Good God! Look at that traffic!"

There were a couple of times on the way downtown when I
thought Felix would get out and walk. He swore every time we missed
a traffic light and glared at vehicles that got in front of our cab.

"Good old Eleanor," he would suddenly murmur. "I'll tell Margot
to raise her pay for this."

Ted, the so-and-so, couldn't resist practicing his surgery on this
budding rupture. "You think it's all settled, do you?"

"Huh? What? Margot's sick, ain't she? The fight's off. You don't
kick a guy when he's down, do you? Or maybe you do. Anyhow,
there's been enough of this siege. Margot was in the wrong—O.K.
She did us out of a swell chance—O.K. The thing now is to forget it.
I'm not saying a word, see? And you two, keep your traps shut. I
ought to dump you out, Ted. But you're her brother and she's terribly
sick. I suppose I have to let you come along. But if you ask her
anything about our row, I'll pop you on the nose. Is that straight?"

Ted tried to look bored. "As you say, tough guy."

By then we had turned off Fifth Avenue into Ninth Street and were
approaching the brownstone house in which they had their apartment. Felix was out of the car almost before it stopped. I followed
right on his heels, and Ted was left to pay the fare.

I heard Margot's delighted, rather impish laughter before I saw her,
and it stopped me, momentarily, on the stairway leading to their
topfloor flat. It confused me. From Felix' account, I had expected to
find her dying; but that laughter—it was so healthy-sounding.

Then I was at the doorway looking in.

There was Margot, facing the doorway. Never had she looked more
beautiful, more *alive*. And how gaily she was laughing—holding out
her arms and laughing.

And there was Felix, startled, dumfounded, groping. He raised his
hands slowly and went toward her. Then made the last stride in a
leap. He had caught the infection of her gaiety.

"Bugs!" That was his name for her. "What the hell! You're supposed to be practically dead. Eleanor . . ."

"Silly! Do I look like double pneumonia? That was a little joke."

Eleanor the colored maid grinned from the doorway behind her
mistress.

Suddenly I was abashed, feeling intrusive. I turned from the entrance, and found Ted sitting dejectedly on the top step. And at that I began to laugh. The old calamity howler was taking a licking.

"Ask Margot if she has a drink," he said, without looking up.

Becoming aware of us in the hall, she called out: "Come in, boys. The party's about to begin." She met us at the doorway.

She turned to Felix. "It's a dirty trick, honey boy, but after all, you have it coming." She slipped her hand through his arm, smiling up at him. We wondered what was up.

Until then, we had been in a long and rather narrow entrance hall, with blue walls and copper-on-white furniture. On one side were the living quarters, on the other the bedrooms. Margot was leading us into the living room, all of us puzzled, watching her.

The living room was large. There was a fireplace with a mirror over the mantel reaching almost to the ceiling. A grand piano triangled the far corner. The furniture upholstery was in leather or bold new fabrics. Everything looked liveable, and expensive.

But the most interesting object in the room at the moment was the man standing just in front of the fireplace, his hands in the coat pockets, who took a slow stride toward us as we entered. He was slightly bald, slightly pudgy, and very successful-looking. He wore eye glasses on a black cord and white piping on his waistcoat.

"Mr. Smith," Margot was intoning in the strong voice of a tragic actress at the big moment of a play. "Mr. Hadley Smith. You know Mr. Cavendish, my husband. And this is my brother, Mr. Rogers, and this is Mr. George, an old friend."

How she kept from laughing was a puzzle. Her eyes were fairly popping with her well devised mischief.

Felix was something of an actor himself, yet hardly adequate to the moment. He couldn't quite laugh, couldn't quite say anything; in fact, could only shake hands and make a noise in his throat.

"Let's all have a drink," Margot sang out, like a school girl on holiday. Eleanor was already coming out of the kitchen with a tray full of dry martinis, as if she were playing a well rehearsed part in a play and had heard her cue.

When we finished the first one, getting by on weather talk, and Margot had poured out the second drink, she played her finesse and left us gaping.

"Mr. Smith wants to get a peep at the play. He called me this morning and I told him when I expected you so we could all be here." She was as innocent as a lamb.

"One happy family," Ted jibed, giving me a baleful look.

Smith, a little embarrassed, I thought, tried to set things straight. "Sorry about the other day, Mr. Cavendish. It was a busy day and my mind wasn't on things. . . ."

At that Felix roared, all pleased, all charmed with everything, but above all with Margot. "You mean you got in on one of Margot's seances. When you know her better, you'll find that one of her most charming traits." He smiled sweetly upon all of us, as if he had never in his life thought otherwise.

"I can imagine," Mr. Smith replied, beginning to feel at home. He had finished his second drink and was cutting the end off of a cigar with a gold clipper. "Of course, it would have suited me better if the lady had got a better line on me. She was, I'd say, a little hasty." The cigar was rolling clouds of smoke into the room and Mr. Smith was rocking back and forth on his pudgy feet, hands behind his back.

"But I must have been pretty close to right, Mr. Smith," Margot spoke up, not letting anything get by. "Otherwise, would you have called me? Honor bright?"

The cigar rolled a bit, smoke billowed. "Oh, now. Called you? Is that the way you took it? Oh, no, Mrs. Cavendish. Oh, no."

Felix had stopped smiling, his eyes opening wide. I looked at him, then at Margot, and wondered what was coming next. "Let's talk about the play, Mr. Smith. The play's the thing. Margot, how about another drink?" He reached out to take her hand, but Margot eluded him.

"Mr. Smith was saying I had been hasty," she observed, unperturbed by the storm signals beginning to fly. "I didn't finish all I might have said, but that wasn't haste on my part. There's one thing I can add now. Just this, that you know yourself pretty well, Mr. Smith, maybe better than most people, but you're an ostrich when it comes to admitting unlovely traits. You know I'm right about your being afraid of yourself—but be-damned if you'll admit it. Do I score another hit?"

"Margot, you dunce!" Felix blurted out. "Let's have another drink. Mr. Smith came to discuss the play, not himself."

"That's what you think," she shot back. "But he really came because he knows I can set him straight about himself. That's what he needs, just that, to get set straight about himself. He thinks the theater is going to do it—but that's a boyhood fantasy. At bottom, secretly, he knows it. He knows he's in for a big flop. And wants to be saved. That's why he came, you goose."

"Margot, you insufferable ninny! For once in your life stop being cute! You bore me to death."

By then Felix was getting in stride to pace the floor, while Margot pulled her familiar trick of speaking with utter calm and wearing an air of insulted innocence. Hadley Smith stood by, his cigar drooping, his jauntiness gone. I couldn't tell whether he was angry or be-wildered or embarrassed. For all that showed on his face, he might have been secretly enjoying himself. As for Ted, I could feel him grinning through the back of my head. I didn't turn.

"If you're bored, Felix, why don't you take a walk? It may cheer you up."

"Margot, don't let's get into a row! Let's be calm and reasonable."

"You're so amusing, Felix. The way you work yourself into a froth and then ask me to be calm. Really! Go look at yourself in the mirror."

Felix had to pace the floor in earnest after that crack.

"You're impossible! Stubborn! Intolerable! Narrow minded! Self-ish! A piece of baggage!"

"And you, darling, are a big piece of stale cheese! And you have flat feet besides!"

"You—you! With your garbling of other people's lives! You're a pink-eyed nanny goat always chewing somebody's wash! You . . ."

That was too much. That was the stroke which broke down Margot's armor of restraint. She got quite wild and marched right at Felix looking murderous. Her fingers clawed. And he, always know-ing when he had gone too far, began to back away. The faster she charged, the faster was his retreat.

"Get out!" she kept shouting. "Get out!"

"Now, listen, Margot . . ."

"Get out, you cluck!"

"Ah, Buggsy!"

"Get out!"

They were at the doorway. She lunged at him, but he had whirled out of reach. Then, convinced that he could not reason with her, Felix dashed for the stairway. Margot was not satisfied with that. She had not spent herself.

"Don't come back!" she shouted, and to emphasize her displeasure she snatched up the first thing that came to hand—which happened to be a bowl of flowers, water and all. She hurled it down the stairwell. We heard the splintering crash, the slop of water.

Felix wailed. "Margot, you got me all wet!"

"You were born that way," she screeched back.

Coming back into the room, her mouth began to waver. Her face got long and lugubrious. Tears sparkled. She reached out and, finding my shoulder convenient, burst out crying.

"He-he-he didn't give me a-a-a chance to te-tell him how lone-some-lonesome I-I-I've been," she wailed.

We all felt miserable. And there wasn't a drink in sight.

And then Smith, silent all that while, began to rock back and forth on his pudgy feet once more. He had taken out a fresh cigar to light.

"Mrs. Cavendish," he remarked, nonchalantly, "this whole affair, amusing as it has been, was unnecessary. We got off on the wrong foot and—well, things went from bad to worse. Let me explain why I came up here. I suppose you know I'm looking for plays—good plays. I'm paying money for them and I mean to get my money's worth. So much for that. When you and Mr. Cavendish . . ."

"Call him Felix. Mr. Cavendish sounds like his father," Margot interrupted, sniffling a little. "And call me Margot. It sounds like myself."

"As you like. When you and Felix called on me the other day I had looked you up carefully. Nobody enters my office that I don't know something about. It's an old habit from downtown. I knew what you could deliver, and to be frank with you, I was pretty anxious to see your stuff. And then you sidetracked the interview. It's a bad habit of yours, I was warned. So when it happened, I wasn't surprised."

He stopped and smiled all around. The man was evidently more than a checkbook. He might even be likeable. We drew closer.

"I was really busy that day and had to cut you off. After all, we weren't getting anywhere. What I could have told you, if I hadn't been in a hurry, was that the stories you read about me were the bunk. That thing about me nursing an old nostalgia for the stage is poppy-cock. Pure and simple poppy-cock. I have a theory that a man should change his business at least once every ten years. It keeps him alive. I've made three or four changes already. Wall Street was the last stop. Now, it's the theater. You missed me by a scalper's margin when you guessed that the Street had been dull and dreary and I was escaping from it. Hell, it's the most exciting place in the world, even with normal blood pressure. You were wrong about other things, too. For example, that dizzy blond angle—hell, there have been plenty of those. . . ."

"Oh, my God! Catch me!" Margot whooped, feigning a swoon into her brother's arms.

"And now, Mrs. Cavendish—Margot—won't you please let me see that play you have ready? The dialogue is probably worthless, if you supplied it, but maybe we can redeem it. . . ."

"Worthless! It's the best dialogue in three seasons! Felix says so. And where *is* Felix?" Her face began to look long and lugubrious again.

She turned accusingly upon Smith. "Why did you let him get away? You bum! You let me say all that tripe, and now he's gone! After I spent a week scheming to get him back. . . ."

I was holding her against my shoulder once more, and looking sideways I caught a glance of Ted, the old vulture, sneaking towards the door. He had had more than his black heart could stand.

From the doorway he shouted back: "I'm going out to get a drink. Then I'm going to swallow prussic acid to take the sweet taste out of my mouth and start on a world cruise in a canoe. When I reach the Scilly Isles I'll send you two a comic valentine."

"If you should fall and break your neck," I shouted back, "let the carcass lay, won't you?"

At that moment, I decided to get married.

Let the War Be Fought

▷ ▷ ▷   Southward, and southward. Red clay flashing from highway cuts.

"Into the bowels. The bowels." These were the shuttling words which wove patternlessly in Matthews' head as he thrust foot to accelerator. Southward, and southward. Into the bowels. Bo-o-o-wels, the motor crooned, as his foot went down hard and the little car arched over a hill. Then red flash of highway cut. *Bo-o-o-wels.* Zo-o-om-m.

Matthews had a squirrel-cage mind, spinning and spinning. He was driving South for the first time, and naturally he thought *South.* Poor white trash. Mammy at the wisteria door. Jim Crow. "Way Down Upon the, etc." (he tried to get that one out of the picture). Magnolias. Magnolias. Magnoli . . . Poor white trash. Mammy with a bandanna head. Jim Crow. "Way Down . . ." He went like that for hours, a marathon revolver, or revolutionist. It came naturally. He could keep it up the day long and be none the worse for it. "Just like a squirrel," he addressed himself, hearing his head refraining "Way Down Upon the . . ."

Before he knew it he was at Greensboro—or was it Greensville? or Greentree? No, Greensboro, N.C. And he knew he was in the South for sure because when he talked to a lady in the public library about looking up something on the Civil War she pulled the draw string in her lips, puckered at him.

"That's your way of putting it, Sir. I'm a Daughter of the Confederacy. We say the *Confederacy War*."

"Yes, ma'm, and you're quite right." Matthews backed away then and decided that it wasn't worth while looking up anything on the Civil and/or Confederacy War. Just then he was a vacationist. He would stick to his list. Let the war be fought.

In Virginia the day before, it had snowed, February snow. Now, bearing down toward the South Carolina line, spring was coming with a rush. He opened the car window and nosed at the sun-drenched air. Indubitable spring. Confederacy War! Why wasn't old purse lips out with her sniffer! Blue sky. Golden sun. Trees in a green haze. Hills coming at him, making the car heave upward. Pines— would they be Loblolly pines?

Matthews was satisfied, breathed deeply. "This is my feast! Let the war be fought!"

He would be called good looking, because lean, six-foot, pleasant-faced men always are. He was getting towards forty. Not there yet, you know, but inching along. Hair was thinning, but his eyes (gray, by the way) were unensacked by fatigue, and in fifteen years he hadn't broken in a new notch on his belt. He was a New Yorker, and a publisher, and you could say of him, candidly, that he knew his way around.

It was vacation time for Matthews, the first in three years (the black years, when book-buyers had been devoured by locusts). With spring coming on, the Old Man of Hurley & Son, "publishers since 1840," had clapped him on the shoulder after a good lunch. "Jack, your eyes are looking squidgy. New York's bleached you out. Drive yourself down to Florida. Take your time, nose around. Get tanned up." Matthews had misgivings. Introspectively, he wondered if he had slackened up and if the Old Man was dropping the first brick on his toe. Then he decided, recovering, that he must be tired. It was only when tired that he feared the devil. And therefore the vacation was the thing.

He drove southward, feasting on the sun.

Magnolias. Magnoli . . . Loblolly pines. (Where but in the South would they think up Loblolly?)

This was the second day of driving and he was still squirreling in the same cage.

It was at Greensboro, stopping for a look around, that purse-lips set him up about the Confederacy War, and it was on the highway below Greensboro that, sticking to the figure, he opened a little door in the cage and got himself straightened out. The thing about Matthews was that, when the right time came, he could always spring the door in the barrel of his head and walk out.

A red-headed girl started it. A red-headed girl standing at the roadside, waiting for a pick-up. He happened to be the one.

He had been thinking of how the wind had stiffened—it had begun to tear at the car, making it lurch startlingly, and to whistle into the fissure he had left open for air. Then when he saw the girl standing at the roadside, her red hair streaming from behind over her eyes, he thought of it again. "The wind is blowing. . . ."

She raised her hand, indecisively, but wittingly. The sun, at her back, glazed his windshield and she could not make out what might be behind the wheel, he surmised. And as his car slowed he reminded himself that toughness was the thing with a broad.

He helped with the indoor handle, and she stood framed in the opening. She wore a frayed green cloth coat with skimpy fur around neck and cuffs. She was looking up, taking him in, her gray eyes expressing the animation of a buried soul (the phrase flashed aptly)— buried soul in Carolina. Then she stepped in and crossed her long thin legs. No more than that.

He tried an ironical approach. "You're the first thumber I've stopped for—and I've passed up a couple dozen. All men. That's what sex does."

The apathetic eyes turned toward him, without an accompanying appreciative smile. *Tenebrae factae sunt.* Perhaps she was dim-witted! Perhaps she was in twilight! Darkness descended in the ninth hour, the chant went. She had faced forward again.

"I reckon a woman finds it plenty hard anyhow she does." These, her first connected words, left him smiling. So! She expected to weep her way past the patrol! That was how she had sized him up!

"You find it hard to be a woman, do you? Let me tell you something, a secret. . . ." He paused, and saw her take her eyes from the road and glance uncertainly at him. "It's hard at times being a man."

Her eyes flashed on him full, fleetingly, and then she went to road staring again.

He restored impersonality by asking how far she was going. "Down heah a piece." She mentioned a town near the South Carolina border. "You go that fa'?"

"Yeh, and farther."

She was stirring a bit, putting her hair to rights, clipping bobby-pins on the frayed edges. Her raw wrists flexed prominently. She was over-rouged. He could imagine her apathetic make-up art, practiced before a mirror fragment, as she got herself ready for the highway. Daily business. How did she make out?

"Looking for work?" The question had its hazards. She might turn on the tears.

Her face went set. Her skin was country skin, ungroomed, perhaps unwashed in a week. The rouge, he saw, looking closer, lay patched on the cheeks like a swipe of white wash on weathered board. She was gangling-limbed. Her nails were broken, undergrimed. Working hands, and no work. The highway—could one say highway-walking? Didn't sound like anything.

"Mill down heah's sta'ting again, they tells me. To'nado busted it last spring and I ain't wo'ked since. Jest been told about it. Sho hopes they puts me on."

"Do you hitch rides often?" Once he had noticed her hands, his eyes kept returning to them. How long did working hands look like working hands after work stopped?

" 'Tain't often I leaves home. 'Cept when I goes looking up a job."

He frowned. Those hands were getting in the way. They were boiled-lobster red with fine muddy cracks. They looked stiff. There would be no more questions, he decided; and then, almost at once, asked another.

"What if they don't put you on—then what?"

"I don't just know. There has to be something, 'cause I needs it so bad."

"Well, what's your name?"

"Loreller May. Loreller May Boggs. See!" He frowned again. She went too eagerly into her worn handbag to fish out from among her trash some kind of official looking card. It turned out to be a driver's license, a year old, of the State of North Carolina. See!" She pushed it at him. It was her best gag.

LORELLA MAY BOGG. AGE, TWENTY-TWO (IN 1935).
SEX, FEMALE. HEIGHT, 5 FT. 5 IN. WEIGHT, 122 LBS.
EYES, GRAY. HAIR, BROWN (RED IN 1936).

"We ain't got no autor now. It was nigh falling to pieces when we got it. That was befo' the to'nado when I was wo'king I bought it fo' ma cause it's troublesome fo' he' to get around. I carries this in case I get kilt and they'll know who it is."

She had him swaying. It was the red hands he kept telling himself. Big City man falls for country girl's story, he telegraphed himself. When you get out of the Big City, he reflected sourly, you can be made to believe anything you're told. City provincialism.

Lorella May was saying something, staring straight ahead as she spoke. She had the dullest voice he remembered ever hearing.

"I don't know what you'd think of me if you was to know what I got to do tonight."

He wasn't properly listening, he was so occupied with figuring her out. She had to repeat the sense of her words.

"I'm sure you wouldn't think good of me if I was to tell you."

That brought him around with a start. Of all the silly-sillys! Was the girl really taking him for a ride?

"Listen, sister! Move over. Your hoopskirts are pinching my leg." He saw her give him a startled look.

"I mean stop talking with your mouth full. If you're going out selling your wares, say so. I can take it."

Her eyes were large as she turned full gaze upon him. She wasn't bad to look at when her apathy was shed. By side glancing at her he could see her taking his words apart and looking for the sense.

His city smartness was too much. She gave it up and went her own way. "Don't judge me hard, mister. I got to do it. It's fo' ma, because she's got to have the medicines. She's po'ly, and I got to do it, honest, mister. It's not that I want to, like you maybe think."

Then she was apathetic again, slumped back in the seat. "I needs money mighty bad—two dolla's sixty cents is what I needs."

"How do you figure the sixty cents? Sounds like bargain week in the basement store."

"I just figure it that way. Takes about that amount fo' ma's needs—flour and fatback and medicines. There's just three things I won't do fo' to get it."

"Three things?"

"I feel mighty shameful telling you this, mister, but I might's well—steal it, kill somebody fo' it, or go with a nigger."

"Hm." Matthews knew that he wouldn't have to ask any more leading questions. It was all coming out.

"I swear, mister, I sho needs that money. I wants to get that stuff fo' ma so I can leave her whilst I get me that job at the mill. There's lots a places along this road where there ain't nobody to watch."

Matthews had a curious sensation which he fumbled to discover. He probed himself. And then he realized, and was dismayed, that he was blushing. City provincialism again.

"Well—it's plain what you mean," he stuttered.

The girl, unconscious of his panic, drove at him again. "I sho needs that money, and they ain't nothin' I wouldn't do fo' it, except as I tells you, them three things. It's fo' my ma, mister, and I hope you don't feel bad about my askin' it."

Matthews' embarrassment did not lessen. Fact was, he had to admit, he didn't know how to take the girl. She played the game on a hick-level and expected him to dish out two bucks sixty. That was enough to make anybody from the Big City burn up. But the girl had him stopped. The simplicity of it knocked him off stride.

"Are you kidding me?" He threw all the emphasis he could into the words, trying to make her believe that she was playing with hot stuff.

At that she eyed him, apathetically, buried soul (he remembered the phrase again). "I'd like fo' you to see ma. She's in po' shape. You could drive home and see fo' yo'self."

"Forget it. Maybe you're on the level. Maybe not." Then he looked at her more coolly—frazzled hair that had been brown last year and now smoldered in a dozen shades of rusty red; dry rouged skin, freckles over the nose; and slumped, inelastic shoulders—she was trying to make these her stock in trade.

"Sister, I don't doubt your needing money. Whether it's for your ma or yourself, you probably need it. But I'm not interested in anything *you* can sell me."

That produced silence. She didn't protest, only stared straight ahead. Her shoulders, possibly, slumped an inch lower. He watched her sidewise. Sunlight, pouring in upon her, was prismed in a tear drop. He caught the glint of it, and felt himself grow heavy. His words, then, had jabbed home. She was sentient. He waited while she made a stealthy move of her hand across her face to rub out the brimming moisture. She also squeezed her nose between fingers, and he guessed that she had no handkerchief. He felt heavier.

Southward, and southward. Red earth still flashing. Poor white trash . . .

"I didn't mean to be personal," he spoke almost tenderly. "If you want something to eat, and you probably do, I'll feed you when we strike a restaurant."

Her reply dragged out. "Thanks, mister. I couldn't eat nothing."

"Don't be silly. You have to eat, whatever happens. And there won't be any strings attached to it. Have you had dinner?"

"I had a bite this morning. But I don't want nothing. I'll get out soon's we get to town. It ain't fa' now, just around the next curve."

He slowed down as they were rounding the curve, and there before them were the first roof tops and a scattering of decaying sheds. He let the car roll off the pavement on to a widened parking and slipped it out of gear. The brake pulled the car down to a soft stop and the motor fell into a whisper.

He picked up her idle hand, turned it palm upward and searched the roughened surface. There was no joking about a hand like that.

"I don't know yet whether your game's on the level or not," he said, smiling as if he were her uncle. "I'm not taking you up so it doesn't matter. If I knew you were stringing me, I don't mind telling you I'd slap your ears off. On the other hand, if you're in a jam and have to do this as a way out, you're stuck. With your—temperament's the word—you'll be a flop."

She turned her dead-soul eyes on him and he had to stop. She knew as well as he, he guessed, that she wasn't qualified for the job and in her dumb way she was begging him to lay off. He still held her hand, which lay inert and barely warm. He was trying to get a picture of her that would explain her and the magnolias.

"Lorella, do you say Civil War or Confederacy War?"

She brought her eyes up to him again and only stared. She could make no sense out of the question, as he expected.

"I can't see it." He wasn't talking to her, rather he was puzzling to himself. "I can't see it. What if the mill does put you on, taking you at your word that that's what you want. I don't see what six-seven bucks a week gets you. And if you're not on the level about looking for a job, this highway business is no cinch for you."

He caught himself up, squeezed her hand, and smiled. "You think I'm buggy, don't you? Well, I am. I'll give you a buck and you can try your luck with another guy. I'll drive you in."

The car rolled onward, spurted to let the gears climb, then as it settled into the high the tires sang plausibly to the pavement.

Matthews followed the highway markers into town and went past the nest of business buildings where the town breathed. Curious, penetrating gazes pressed upon him. Native eyes always produced a slight psychic disturbance in him, he had noticed, when he drove slowly through a waiting and watching town, but in that place the effect seemed to be stronger than ever. He turned mildly red and watched the road. Then he realized what was happening. They were looking at the girl. They knew her. He watched her through the tail of his eye as he pulled toward the curb.

"Not here," the girl said quickly, under breath. "Go down a couple squares, will you?"

The impression grew into conviction that the girl was known in town, but he checked an impulse to lay her by the heels. Naturally, she couldn't very well work the highway round about without becoming known. As his softness toward her ebbed away it left him cold and angry. But he handed her the buck.

"On second thought," he remarked sourly, "you probably make out pretty well. What does the story matter that you cook up, just so you collect. Soft guys always come along."

They were at the curb, she hesitating, with her hand on the door lever. "Don't think bad of me, mister. I needs it, honest."

She tried that look of innocence again, tears in the eyelashes, dumb and simple. One long leg was thrusting through the door, while her raw, awkward hands fumbled to get the dollar bill into her purse.

He flamed up, angered by his own imbecility rather than by her country art. "I'm getting tired of that weepy look, sister. Please take it away."

She slid and crawled out of the car, trying to say something, but not succeeding. On the sidewalk she pulled herself together and, though he tried not to look at her again, he could not help but notice how string thin she was, and how slumped.

Then he was squirreling once more. Magnolias. Magnoli . . . Poor white trash. That's to say, he was wordless, empty of the connective tissue of thought. He spun. And gaping, he watched the girl go down the street.

She went cross-lot before she reached the corner. It was instinct for her to do that, even though she must have been aware of his watching her, of his realizing she was at home. He watched, fascinated, enraged. Dumb as she looked, she had got away with it!

He reached for the door handle, to open the door and pull it securely to. Opening the door let daylight in upon the floor boards. His eyes opened wide. Unbelieving. He bent closer. There lay the dollar bill. He remembered her awkward fumbling with her purse when he handed her the money. She had somehow missed the opening. His anger had confused her.

He looked up in time to see the girl turn right and disappear in a street of sagging frame houses. At first he smiled. Then he frowned. Then he glowered.

"Of all the dumb luck!"

He put the car in motion, slowed at the first intersection, and turned left. He was going to restore her property.

"A Christian gentleman," he thought, with a wry sag of the lip corners.

A right hand turn. Now to find her. No one in sight. On each side of the rutted street were workmen's houses. No mistaking them, no describing them, always alike. When paint gives out, all boards look alike. When window lights go, rags will keep out the frost. When beams rot, all houses go earthward.

Midway in the block he rolled to the curb and got out. Children were appearing in opening doors. Heads thrust at him. Dirty faces masked inner wonder.

"Sonny, I'm looking for a young woman, just came down this street. She lost something. I want to give it to her."

After several efforts, he found a wordless hand pointing out a house, as window-broken and out of joint as the others. Of course there would be no bell, he reminded himself after a moment's search of the doorway. You don't need doorbells when you don't leave calling cards.

It was preposterous, what he was doing. He shouldn't have started on this trip without a guardian.

He wasn't sure that he was asked in. The house seemed lifeless. But presuming that his knock was welcome, he entered, first a dark hall, then an open doorway on his right.

There he stood voiceless, witless. Magnolias and wisteria and poor white trash. Wouldn't he ever get the thing straight!

The girl sat full-facing him, coatless now—coat, bag and hat lay tossed upon a buckling bed. The room was in twilight, yet he could see her plainly. Her dress was opened to her full breast and an infant lay in her bending arm, drowsily feeding. In the deeper shadows behind her chair a boy of about two stood shyly on one foot. He saw it plainly.

"You—dropped this." It was as if his voice were in a valley and he on a mountain top. It strained to be audible, but only a whisper got to him. "As a matter of fact, where did I put it?" The question was a stall, since he had just put the dollar bill out of sight.

"Well, I'm silly. Put it back in my billfold. Here it is. I'll lay it on the table. Don't get up. I have to go."

At the doorway he looked back, warmed up now. He was no longer afraid of himself or of the girl. "You shouldn't have pulled that old mother story. You had a better one." He grinned at her. The twilight hid her eyes, thank God!

Before he reached the walk he heard her calling "Mister! Mister! You left five dollars!" He had hoped to get beyond earshot. He hurried.

Now southward again. Magnolias and wisteria and Loblolly pine. Where but in the South. . . .

In the Alien Corn

▷ ▷ ▷   When people speak in my hearing of a career in music, I shudder. It is not reasonable; such careers need not have the beginnings I associate with them. Just the same, I think back and shudder.

The very first time I met Mrs. Niles I heard her tell two bustling ladies from Marietta, Ohio, who had come to make eyes at her suddenly famous sons: "I've brought the boys almost six thousand miles for their chance in Paris. Now they're here, nothing will interfere with their work."

When Mrs. Niles talked to you, she drilled you. The dark points of her eyes penetrated. Her short slender body was always rigid, sitting or standing. She never smiled.

The women from Marietta had come to say how wonderful it would be if the boys would give a joint recital at their Club, Nelson playing some of David's compositions. Mrs. Niles stared them down.

"They have quite enough work as it is."

I thought then that if I ever had to disagree with Mrs. Niles I would do it by letter. She was too concentrated. Her gray hair gave a false impression of her vigor.

Then she was backing the two clubwomen out of the room. They were suddenly lame and furious. They nodded and smiled and said

"Not at all. We quite understand," but they had spots of color right under their eyes.

I decided, ingenuously, to show Mrs. Niles that I sympathized. "Maybe they'll think of such things before they ask any one again."

She looked at me. I had been introduced to her just half an hour before by her son Nelson. Now she looked at me as if seeing me for the first time. Then she walked away.

When I began visiting the Niles' apartment in the Rue St. Dominique, Claudia was away. I would never have gone back after that first time, and maybe never have met her, if Nelson had not urged me and looked distressed when I showed unwillingness. He was a pleasant boy, utterly naive, but warm-hearted and anxious to have friends. "Mother isn't cheery, but she's all right. She'll do anything for us. Do come along." I could have told him that we had nothing in common, and I had no reason why I should get myself punctured by a stare, but I didn't. He was too mild and pleasant. I went along.

I had been going there a month before I met Claudia. It was a winter night. The rain had been coming down like a spillway long enough to have washed clean every stone in Paris. The gutters ran clear water. In such rain one paid the cabdriver before opening the door and then, committed to it, bounded like a rabbit for the protection of the doorway.

I wasn't thinking of Claudia as I began the long spiralling climb to the top floor. At that moment I knew only her name. It was so with everybody. They knew her brothers, or had seen their names in the American newspapers, and Claudia existed only as a member of the family.

Nelson, the elder, had come along two years before with a scholarship at Fontainebleau and since then had been winning every prize put up. And he was not yet twenty-one. At his debut the preceding spring his name got beyond the music notes and bobbed up in the editorial page of one Paris edition.

Since the autumn however the younger brother, seventeen-year-old David, had been pushing Nelson to one side and getting the play for himself, as a composer. His songs were being heard in small salons. A ballet was in rehearsal. There was talk of a symphony in process.

It was of these two that I was thinking as I paused after the third flight and took wind for the last twenty steps (I had counted them before). And I was thinking too of the mother of these boys. How would she treat me tonight—would she be insulting, or would she be kind enough to ignore me?

When I entered the room and saw Claudia I forgot all that.

They liked a subdued light in that family and I recall the room only vaguely. It was large, the ceiling was high, and the colors were red and white; light gray walls and white trim, red drapes pulled partly across the tall windows, and red carpets. There was a large table somewhere in the room, a number of curved-leg chairs, bookcases and mirrors. Then there was a fireplace, no doubt a marble mantle. In front of the fireplace a great stuffed sofa, reminding one of a hippopotamus heaving its back out of a waterhole. It had an offspring, a fat chair turned at an angle to the hearth and partly facing the sofa. Claudia was in that chair, her feet tucked under her. There must have been a fire in the grate because one side of her glowed.

I am not sure who met me at the door but it must have been Nelson. It usually was.

"This is Claudia. She's been away."

What one says at such a moment is rarely important, but even if it were a gem of pleasantry, it would be forgotten afterward. I probably stared and mumbled. And somehow I got to the corner of the sofa next to her chair.

It wasn't anything about her looks that made me so aware of the last twenty steps I had just climbed. Or not entirely her looks. Whatever it was, it was all one. Face and body and dress, and how she looked when she talked, or how she sat and watched the fire. Her dress was white and simple, a kind of woven wool stuff. She wore a silver brooch with a turquoise stone. Her dark hair was done in a braid around her head. That much I remember.

She woke me up. "I suppose you're one of the crowd that's been keeping my brothers from touching earth."

"Why . . ." I found myself crumbling. "I've been thinking they do pretty well. They take it quietly."

She watched me. "You've been Nelson's special friend, I hear. Did he pick you?"

The crumbling was completed. Then I rallied. "See here," I said. "If you want information. . . . You know my name, Pip Stevens, nickname, of course. Twenty-eight, unmarried, Westerner. I know nothing about music. I'd be satisfied with an accordion."

She smiled drearily. "I was only curious about Nelson. He's never had an older friend. Maybe he's beginning to grow."

Nelson joined us then, coming from across the room and bringing one of the friends Claudia probably had in mind—this was a fair-haired boy looking much younger than he doubtless was, whose squeaky voice caused one to look up in surprise. I had been seeing him lately too. In fact, one never saw Nelson without almost surely seeing the blond Cedric.

I had met Nelson some months before at the Student Union and had asked him to drop around to my hotel when I learned that he was from Montana. Then I forgot about it. When he did come some weeks later, I hardly remembered him; then he asked if he might come again and bring a friend. For weeks now he had been visiting me regularly, Cedric with him. Neither ever came alone. Neither, I decided, came to see me. But this had all started before I ever came to the Niles apartment or knew about the preoccupation with music.

The talk rolled along, with Claudia and me left behind. I saw her trying to make sense out of their chatter. I had tried it and knew that it was useless. A remark from me always went unnoticed. They talked of inconsequential matters—whether a certain mutual acquaintance was being favored by their piano teacher; whether the approaching debut of still another acquaintance would attract attention; whether a meat diet gave one's fingers extra strength. Claudia smiled at some of their remarks, but when she interrupted the reaction was what I expected—a kind of surprised silence. Then she looked at me and I could see she was wondering why I didn't take a hand, since Nelson was supposed to have made a friend of me. She wanted the fair-haired Cedric squelched. But I knew that, if Cedric was to be squelched, I was not the one to do it.

Finally we managed an undertone conversation of our own.

"You've been south?" I asked her.

"For a month, fact-gathering. Did you know that in the last two years the silk trade at Lyons has fallen off alarmingly?"

"No, I didn't know that. Wonderful, isn't it?"

"Wonderful?" From her puzzled look I saw that I had miscued. She was serious, but how was I to know? Then I heard her laugh for the first time.

"Tell me," I said. "Did you know . . ." I nodded in Cedric's direction, "before you went away?"

"No. He's a new one."

"Well, they come and drink up my tea."

More could have been said about that, but the moment was lost. We had all heard the door open and we all turned. Then we rose to our feet.

It was Mrs. Niles, that strange creature. She came in like a sleep-walker, her face expressionless, her movements tranced. It was somebody's idea, probably her own, of the grand manner in drawing room entrances. It froze everybody (for all I knew, that might be what was supposed to happen when a lady entered a drawing room, but it seemed on the stiff side). She was well into the room before she glanced around to see who was there. We three who had been seated on the couch made way for her. She chose the middle and motioned Nelson to the place at her right. This left the left side free and I could see that Cedric was preparing to preempt the place, where I had been sitting. He was most welcome. But Mrs. Niles was intent on having herself surrounded by her family.

"David," she called out without turning her head. "Why do you sit back there always reading? Come sit here with us."

Until then the younger boy had been no part of our circle. He had raised his head and smiled when I entered, and then had resumed his reading. Just then, if I remember, he had come upon Draper's "Intellectual History" and every evening that I saw him he was absorbed in it. The contrast between him and Nelson was striking, and nothing indicated the difference better than the way they cut their hair. Nelson had adopted a romantic pompadour, what is sometimes called a leonine mane; but David's hair was cropped short. There were no airs about him; he spoke but little and what he said sounded sensible. Now when his mother called him he left his book without a protest.

But for David's surprising maturity we would all have sat and stared dumbly. He alone seemed undisturbed by the acid of his mother's tongue.

"Say, Pip, tell us about the Benjamin Franklin letters you've been digging up. I'd like to know history."

The history I knew could be lost in a boar's ear, but David had a pleasant way of addressing me as a chaired professor instead of the graduate student hack that I was.

For a moment I left myself unguarded. David was interested in history and I began to ask what he had read and to suggest other books. The colloquy soon expired.

Mrs. Niles turned to me with lifted brows. "David has enough to do, Mr. . . ." She had been told my name several times.

"Stevens, Mother." David frowned at her.

"My boys," she went on without noticing him, "are interested only in music. They should not be distracted."

"Reading history's no distraction," David could always speak up without starting a row. Mrs. Niles controlled him by ignoring him. She let him say what he wished and then pretended that he was too young to be taken seriously. His good nature kept him from protesting.

Mrs. Niles ended the discussion. "I have the migraine again. You'll have to excuse me, children."

After that we all stood up again, except Claudia. As Mrs. Niles passed, I was aware of the small bright eyes, the thin-lipped mouth. She wore skirt and shirtwaist, a band of black velvet around her throat. I remembered the costume from my childhood. With her hand on the knob she paused, turned halfway to the room.

"It's time for bed, children." She closed the door without a sound.

When she had gone, so many deep breaths were expired that little currents were set up, so I imagined. I found Claudia looking at me and I wondered if she had caught me looking annoyed. Then she smiled.

Later, as I stood in the narrow entranceway getting into my rain-clothes, a curious thing happened. Claudia had followed me and was saying a last word, when I heard a weak, complaining voice come from an inner room. It wasn't a voice I knew and I thought I was acquainted with everyone in the family. I did not intend a question-ing look.

Claudia was embarrassed, I thought. "That's Dad," she explained.

I was so surprised that I paused with my coat half on. "Your father . . . ? I didn't know. . . ."

"Quite true. He isn't often mentioned. An invalid, you know. I wish. . . ." She stopped short. I was sorry.

She had an expressive face, and I could see that she had come to some resolution. "You've met the rest of the family. I'd like you to meet him some day. He's the best of the lot."

"It's agreed!"

The resolution faltered. "We'll see. You'd better not mention it."

She shook hands at that and left me.

$\triangledown$

The meeting with her father came soon afterward.

Claudia called me by telephone one afternoon, and I learned that her mother had accompanied Nelson to his music lesson. I arrived promptly and was shown into her father's back bed-sitting room, a large room overlooking a winter bare garden.

When I entered, her father gave me a fierce look. "If you're another doctor, stay out! If you're one of these piano players, I'm gonna throw you out!"

Claudia giggled at his ferocity. "I've told you about Pip, so behave."

I couldn't say he smiled, but he gave me the fiercest handshake I ever remember receiving, so I guessed I was accepted. He was sitting up in a wheelchair with a gray shawl thrown over his shoulders and his feet thrust into sheepskin moccasins. His nose was high and sharp and his eyebrows were like hedgerows. He was amazingly thin, reminding me of a flat wooden doll held together with string.

"I don't understand piano players," he said without further amenity. "I've been a railroad man most of my years—had a run out of Miles City beginning about the time this young one started growing pigtails. You know the country, I should guess, the wildest damn winters since they locked up hell. If anybody ever tells you the steam froze in midair after leaving the whistle, you can call him a liar, but don't go too strong. I've seen it happen."

"Dad!"

I don't know what Claudia thought I was going to do, the way she looked at me. She should have known better.

"Ever been to Whitefish?" I asked. "But I guess not, since that's on the other railroad. Well, we get a cold snap up there once in a while. We lived kind of in the raw. I remember my mother going to the kitchen door to throw out the dish water. A kind of wind was blowing, and do you know the water came right back at her and blackened her eye? It had turned to ice and broke all over her."

I thought Claudia's father would shake himself right out of the wheelchair. He snorted and choked and finally had to reach for his bandanna handkerchief and blow a blast on his nose. "Best damn story I've heard about Montana since they let sheep in. Oh, my!"

A moment later I was amazed to see his eyes fill with tears. The hair prickled on my neck.

"Excuse me," he mumbled, strangling and swallowing. "These damn pains come over me until I'm like to shame myself. It's this Goddamned rain and chill. I never see such a country for rain in my life."

As if the physical pain reminded him of something else that was always present, he leaned forward. His still gray eyes studied me.

"Since you're a Montana boy, I feel's if I can trust your judgment. You know the boys. D'you think they like what they're doing? Is it what they want to do? I don't see them much. Kate thinks they shouldn't spend much time talking to me. If I get to asking questions, she's always where she can hear and comes and answers for them. What d'you think?"

The gray eyes held me and I did not try to pull away. I answered evasively that the boys probably had not thought much about it. If they had never tried anything else, you couldn't expect them to have any definite notions one way or the other. It seemed to work.

"That's how it is!" he agreed vigorously. "That's what I tell myself. They never had a chance."

Claudia and I were looking at each other, and I saw how close she was to tears. That pull was stronger than her father's eyes. And then, as I sat watching her, she came suddenly alert. She left her father's chair, behind which she had been standing, and walked towards the door.

Mr. Niles continued the thread of his thought. "I've been stewing over this a lot lately. I lie here and think until my head would like to bust. I'm not a thinking man."

Claudia was alarmed. From the door she motioned for silence. Then she opened it slightly. It was unmistakable now. We could hear the scrape of a key.

"It's mother!"

We were like clocks stopped in an earthquake. We stared at each other. Then Mrs. Niles was standing in the doorway. She too stared. Then she turned upon me.

"Mr. Niles is a sick man and isn't to be excited. I thought everybody understood that." When she stepped towards me, I stepped back, then I felt silly. "I can't understand what interest you find in my husband, Mr. . . . ."

"Stevens." I supplied the name for about the twelfth time.

Claudia cut in between us, and I felt even less adequate. "I arranged the meeting," she said casually. "If I had asked you, we would have disagreed and there was no sense in that. The doctor has not forbidden visitors. Well, Dad, I'll run along. You look cheery after seeing a new face." She managed it skillfully, keeping her mother from interrupting, and all the time pushing me toward the door.

In the hallway as I was getting into my coat, Claudia began talking about the Lyons silk trade again. She had written four articles on the subject and just had word that a Philadelphia textile journal had bought the lot.

"As I said before, that's wonderful," I told her.

The remark didn't register, she seemed to be studying. Then she brightened. "On second thought," she said, "I believe I'll come down for a cup of coffee."

▽

Nelson continued to come to my hotel, usually twice a week, in the afternoon, bringing the blond Cedric with him. The boys could have guests at home only on Saturday evenings. How he managed to get these afternoons off puzzled me, but I considered it none of my business to ask.

Claudia decided to take a hand, but she exaggerated my failings as a host. Her complaint was that I put a package of store cookies in the middle of the table and told everybody to go to it. And what was wrong with that? "In the first place, you need to learn how to make tea," she said, changing the subject. "It isn't meant to tan leather or shellac furniture." She went out and bought me some dishes and a variety of trinkets to put on a table when I had guests. I had to carry them home. "The most important thing is to have a slops jar. That's so you don't have to take that last swallow full of twigs you don't know what to do with when you get them in your mouth." I always thought it was all right to pop them out between the teeth.

She had a habit when thinking of standing elbow in hand and a finger tip on her lips, gazing off into space. It made a charming picture. She would stand that way in my room and then she would have an idea. "I know what we'll do for Nelson. I'll bring some girls around. I know some gay things from Connecticut, over here from some female college."

So it was all for Nelson, all this buying of etchings for my room and this instructing me in tea making. But I didn't care. When Nelson came with Cedric and met the Connecticut girls, he almost caved in. Claudia must have anticipated the impulse to panic and run, because she had instructed me to close the door quickly as soon as the boys came inside. Then she made the introductions casually and the boys were trapped with teacups in their hands. It worked out all right. The Connecticut girls knew how to make their eyes burn as they listened to the boys talk and Nelson's pompadour seemed to rear up.

This went on for several weeks and in this time I believe it rained every day. The Seine valley flooded and in Paris itself people stood along the quays and watched the water fill the arches of the bridge. Rats began to leave their cellars. Then it stayed like that, and in another day the newspapers forgot about it and the people went away from the quays.

I saw Claudia almost every day and began to grow used to carrying an umbrella. Left to myself I never bothered to try new eating places or to go hunting out anything which lay off the beaten path. Meeting her changed all that. I had been going to the Bibliotheque and various stuffy archives every day during the fall and early winter, but the zest for smelling out old letters had dissipated. After I had kept up with Claudia for just one week I realized how many things there were to do. I even became interested in ballet.

I made a point also of going to the Niles' every Saturday night. I did not want Mrs. Niles thinking that her manner could frighten me off. Generally she stayed away from our gatherings before the hearth. We talked and laughed, all of us I believe hoping that our gaiety caused her some annoyance. When she did come into the room, we shut up like children visited by the preacher. She walked her solemn way among us and never failed to remind us that it was bedtime.

It could not continue.

One March night, during a lashing rainstorm, Claudia came to my hotel in the Boulevard Raspail. A puddle of water gathered at her feet as she stood in the middle of the tiny public room on the *entresol* while the night porter legged it up four flights to my room to announce the awaiting of a mademoiselle.

"You've got to take off your shoes and have a drink of brandy." For a moment I took her off guard. She looked down at herself and saw the puddle of water. She seemed to smile faintly.

"Never mind. I haven't time. It's nothing." She wet her lips. She looked slack-shouldered.

"I thought it would be decent to warn you that you're in for a row. Then I decided you shouldn't be dragged into it at all. You have nothing to do with it. I'm asking you to leave your hotel, now, tonight. They'll send your stuff later. And after that—" she seemed not quite sure what she meant to follow—"you'd better not see any of us. Don't let Nelson have your address."

I grasped her arm and pulled her to a chair. I sat down beside her. What was it all about? The next moment I forgot what I was going to say because I began to say something entirely unplanned, almost unthought of, except that it couldn't have been.

"What you say is impossible. There's never been any talk between us, but we didn't have to talk. You knew it and I knew it. The first night in your apartment, when I sat down next to you, it was like slipping into a seat meant for me and I've been following you around ever since. Who's going to make a row?"

It was a mixed up statement, but it finally aroused her. She looked alarmed.

"Take my word for it, I can't go away from you." I spoke hurriedly before she interrupted.

She was on her feet, beginning to walk away. "Pip, there's no time to talk like that. I don't know what you're talking about. You haven't listened to me." When I took a step nearer, fearing she would run away before I could reason with her, she really looked frightened.

"Please, Pip! You don't know what you're doing. I can't stay. I wish . . . I wish you had listened." When tears started to her eyes, she ducked her head and ran for the stairs.

If I had been hit by a crowbar, I couldn't have been more stunned. She had come to me in trouble and all I had done was talk about myself! That was pretty stupid. A man couldn't be much stupider. I stood in the middle of the room for perhaps half a minute, though it could have been half an hour, so many things—thoughts, maybe; feelings, yes—chased themselves through my mind. I could not decide whether to follow Claudia or not. How could I repair the blunder?

I hadn't yet moved when I heard the street door slam. That startled me. Claudia must have just gone out. I could catch her! I bounded for the stairs. Then I heard a voice which stopped me cold. Mrs. Niles was down there demanding of René, the porter, that he call me. He would please not argue. She knew perfectly that the hour was late.

A moment later we were staring at each other. My wits did not desert me entirely. A storm was coming and I remembered that there was a second room, a cubbyhole called the *salon de thé,* to which there was a door. The room in which we stood at the top of the landing could not be closed off. I threw on the lights in the *salon de thé* and she entered without speaking.

Then we stared at each other again. She was paler than I remembered ever seeing her.

"I've been trying to explain to myself what you expected to get out of interfering in my family." Her eyes gave me a thorough going over, as if she were really trying to figure out something. I felt kind of naked before she spoke again.

"What reason had you for indulging my sick husband in his child-ish notion that the boys are being held here against their wills? And why have you encouraged my children to practice deceit on me?

Claudia was never my favorite child, but at least she could be trusted. Why have you set yourself against me?"

It sounded mad. "I don't understand. Why do you ask these things?"

She ignored my question. "Has Nelson been visiting you?"

I realized that I had been hoping she would find out, but I had not foreseen how sinister my actions would appear to her.

"Seems like Nelson is old enough to choose his own friends."

The answer infuriated her. A hard glare came over her eyes.

"You were encouraging him to come, and you got him to keep it from me. You and Claudia have been in this together. The boys were supposed to be walking in the Luxembourg. When I could, I went with them. You will say you didn't know that. You'll say you didn't know that when Nelson went to your place, David went off to an art class, some dirty hole in the wall. . . ." She was quite right. The information astonished me.

"Aren't you going to say it? Why hesitate over a few more lies?"

"Mrs. Niles, you'll excuse me. This talk is useless and I'm withdrawing." My getting up and walking to the door had a decisive effect. She was up with me at once and laid her hand on my arm. The belligerent tone was gone and she seemed almost contrite. I turned back to hear what she would say, but I left the door open.

"If I've been unfair, overlook it. I'm terribly upset and may say more than I mean. I hoped to appeal to your understanding, so I came here tonight. When you understand, I know you'll want to help. Our Montana boys play fair."

Maybe she guessed from my expression that this approach was not getting her far. Her voice became solemn.

"If I should lose my boys, after working as I have, I believe I would have to die. That's what I want you to see, if you can. The whole load fell upon me. Mr. Niles never shared it. I don't hold it against him. He did what he could and he worked hard. I washed other people's clothes, kept boarders, made every penny count. He made the burden greater when he began to drink heavily. I'm sure you haven't been told that. We don't speak of it. There were years when I never knew from one day to another what was going to happen to us. Drinking and a railroad job don't go together. If he didn't kill himself,

he might cause the deaths of hundreds of others. I dreaded the day
when he would be found out and fired. It was his brother dying five
years ago and leaving money that made it possible to escape that
dreadful life. I thought when Claudia grew up she would help. She
wasn't gifted in the way the boys were—in her own way she has
talent, I don't misjudge her. But I was wrong in thinking she would
help me. Of course, I let her do as she pleased. I made no demands. . . ."

That was the last I heard. There had been a slight sound just
outside the little room, the door of which was still open. I turned my
head and saw Claudia just crossing the threshold.

Mrs. Niles turned too. I did not see her face but I heard her breath
catch. Then all her calmness was gone. She screamed.

"Claudia!" It was not a name. It was a sound of bitterness and rage,
and something that went beyond even these.

The girl's face held to fixed expression of scorn. "I told you tonight
I wouldn't bother you again, but I didn't count on this. I've seen you
go far to get your way, but lying was beneath you, I thought."

The words stung and brought color to Mrs. Niles' face. "You speak
of lying! You—slut!" Her eyes burned unnaturally. She bore down on
Claudia, using the whole force of her will to silence her daughter. She
was standing quite close when she muttered: "How dare you?"

"Yes, I dare," Claudia's voice was almost inaudible. "You lied about
Father. You lied about me. I heard it all."

Mrs. Niles shrank back as if she had been slapped. Then she threw
herself upon Claudia, her mind beclouded. The hour, the place,
myself all forgotten. She cried incoherently of being "stabbed" and
"shamed."

Claudia was scratched from temple to chin and most of her outer
clothing was torn off before I could get a grip on the raging woman.
She turned upon me, lashed out with her feet, wound her hand in my
hair. I could do no more than hold her and that very awkwardly.
Suddenly she slumped in my arms like a sack of kindling wood. I
looked at her dazedly as she slipped to the floor in an awkward heap.
So we stood, Claudia and I, while heads cleared.

I remember the frightened face of René just outside the door. He
whispered something about "tout le monde" and I seemed to see

blurred faces moving in and out of the little public room. He dashed outdoors for a cab. We followed. Claudia was shaking, turning back to see how I made out. But Mrs. Niles was all but lifeless in my arms. She never moved.

▽

It was morning, and for once it wasn't raining. But it was cold. Fog rolled along, first in the street, then higher up. A doorway would appear, then a dripping tree, then a shining roof. We were drinking black coffee, sitting by a window and looking out.

Claudia tried to smile but her bandaged face was not her own. It would not respond. She reached for my hand.

"Her nerves broke once before," she said, as if in answer to a question. But I had asked nothing. "That was when I refused to quit high school and go to work. She wanted me to sling hash to support the boys. They were dead against it too when they heard. Later, when I could help, it wasn't the same. Now that she's ill, I'll stop hating her. She'll be a person needing help, not my enemy. But I can't cheer yet."

Her hand lay on mine. She wasn't looking at me just then. But in a moment she would be. I waited.

▽

Oh, yes. About the boys. Nelson teaches music in a New Jersey high school, where he takes the band out for marching exercises once a week; while David, who had more substance, returned to Montana. He is now instructor in history at the State University. Very promising student.

Six Beautiful in Paris

▷ ▷ ▷   Waldo Verriman was calculating, with his fine gray eyes slightly squinted and his face turned away from his enthusiastic brother. How inconvenient would it be for him, this chance meeting with the brother who had been "lost" in the West for twenty years? To meet him in Paris, of all places!

"Yes, Rob, we'll have to do that." With what infinite care he let the words slip out! His white teeth cut the words off in chaste portions, his waxed moustache nibbled cautiously. Even so, he had not been careful enough, he realized at once.

"Fine! Wally! Just as I thought. Let's go right away."

One could not mistake it Waldo thought and seemed to wince. He did not look toward neighboring round-topped tables. He did not need to, to know that everybody was looking, that these garçons were standing together, eyebrows lifting. One could not mistake it—his brother had been living out of doors.

"We'll go right up, now!" The voice boomed.

"But . . ." The inner wrist of his right hand resting on the edge of the marble tabletop, Waldo raised his closed fingers upward. That was his only gesture—"it might not be convenient for your family at this hour of the day . . . might not be at home. . . . Besides I really have a luncheon engagement at two. . . . Supposing I call this evening. . . ."

The brothers looked at each other, Waldo calculating, his eyes were open now and looking with studied ease. Robert, the elder, smiling his pleasure even if he did feel slightly nettled. Each began to remember things which in the first moments of excitement on this unexpected meeting in a Rond Point des Champs Elysées café had been forgotten.

Waldo had not changed, that was what Robert noticed. Impeccable Waldo, who, even as a boy, had been careful of his fingernails. With inward mockery, Robert decided that he would have to remind his brother of that—but later, when they got better acquainted. He had been something of a scholar too, had Waldo. Through the long summer days of greedy pleasure away from school dullness, Waldo had kept to his French history, novels and poetry. Everybody counted on him becoming a professor, and he did. By now, he ought to know French inside out. Twenty years had not changed his habits, but they had crowned him with grace. Where before he was precise and well scrubbed, there was now authority in his moustache waxed to a spike and in the margin of starched cuff which flashed upon the eye as he lifted his coffee cup to his waiting pursed lips. Authority, indeed. Citizen of the world. One arm resting on the nub of a walking stick. Waldo Verriman—Professor of Romance Languages. His face had a lovely indoor pallor, his jaw was sharp [. . .], his nose long and narrow, his eyes gray and expressive—the women probably loved him.

Robert remembered all that and could not withhold a cheery sarcasm.

"We don't stand much on ceremony at our house. Come any time it suits you!"

"Thank you, Robert. I'll come along this evening. . . . Say seven-thirty?"

Waldo was bowing, backing away rapidly. As he came up the last time and turned on his heel, the smile which had been shining so pleasantly went flat, as suddenly as a light bulb turned off. Robert watched him settle his gray felt hat at a nice angle as he walked away. He watched the walking stick swing upward, then tap in time with the left stride, moving upward, tap, then, at the street intersection, swing up under the right arm, nub forward. There was authority in that moving of a cane.

Robert smiled to himself, gave his head a quick, admiring shake, and turned in the opposite direction.

▽

It was a difficult evening in every way.

Dinner was eaten in the hotel dining room in the midst of mirror-encrusted pillars and gleaming bare backs, to the accompaniment of digestible music.

Waldo—who was being called Uncle Waldo timidly—came as near to snorting as his impeccability and waxed moustache would permit.

"Do you eat here—always?" He half-paused in sitting down, as if there might yet be a way out.

Lucy, Robert's wife, florid in evening dress, compromised her taste by replying, "Yes, Waldo. Isn't it charming?"

Robert swung to her side, speaking not so boomingly as was his wont: "Not that the people aren't kind of starchy. But it makes you feel like you're seeing the real thing. Continental, Waldo. I guess you know what that is."

Waldo was irritated, bored with himself for having given way to the feeling of family tie. He might have been dining enjoyably in the Rue Cambon—with Julia Apperron. The thought of it increased his irritation.

Robert in his blundering way was asking Waldo to do the honors in ordering the meal. "You can find your way through these French meals better than me, I don't doubt. Let's see what you can do."

"Dining can be an art," Waldo said quietly. It was the first thing he had yet said that gave him any satisfaction.

Robert and Lucy found it necessary to talk a great deal, both of course feeling themselves obliged to let it be known that cattle raising in Montana had not been a bad venture for them; indeed it had given them, while they were still not too old, release from further labor. They had to tell, too, of their son, Ronald, who had been in Paris already two years studying. Ronald thought he would be a writer—and good promise he had, too. The publishers wrote him excellent letters. They were here to spend a few months with him—not to get in his way. They thought he ought to be left alone. He was a good boy and needed no minding. It was part for company's sake they wanted to be near him a while and see what he was planning. And what did Waldo think—the boy was in love! He had written them a bit about the girl, not revealingly, and now they were just discussing that the two were very much in love, thinking of marriage. Except that the girl had ambitions, too, in music, and both were kind of holding back. Yet very much in love.

"It's beautiful, how they're in love!" Lucy said, starry-eyed in the discreet table light.

This talk went on and on, and the meal which Waldo had ordered with such extreme care passed unnoticed through untasting lips. In politeness he asked:

"Who's the girl?"

"Oh, a sweet girl!" Lucy cooed. "Julia Steinberg's the name—from New York."

Waldo looked from Lucy to Robert and stopped eating. He even laid down his fork and with great deliberation wiped his mouth, passing the serviette from the parting in his moustache to the right, then to the left. With great gravity he swallowed the remaining Chablis in his glass and let his eye roam upward to catch the garçon's eye and signal that the glasses should be replenished all around. When the garçon had discreetly withdrawn, he commented:

"Really—is that so? Julia Steinberg—then she's Jewish?"

Now it was Lucy who was surprised into motionlessness. Her blue starry eyes grew large as she returned Waldo's gaze. His tone puzzled her.

"Why, I suppose she is. I never thought of it. She's uncommonly good-looking, I can say that. And they tell me she plays the piano real well."

Waldo returned his attention to his food and the conversation sagged into silence. He took two neat portions of fish before speaking.

"I dare say." He seemed to be unimpressed. "Women of her race are often beauties, when they're young especially."

Lucy and Robert exchanged glances, then Robert tried:

"You seem to have reservations, Waldo—am I right?"

The Silver Locket

I

▷ ▷ ▷   He recalled vividly the scene in the post-office when Marian had given him the locket which he now held in his hand. To the casual observer it could have appeared nothing more than a trinket, rather neatly made, but not at all extraordinary. Nothing to compel a second glance. On one side was a simple arrangement of Greek lines, and on the opposite side the words, "All the Love in the World," and her initials, "M.L."—Marian Lockwood.

Yes, the scene was still fresh in his memory, although it had been, oh—years,—does it matter how many? He had gone down to the post-office, the mail having arrived on the late afternoon train, and while waiting for it to be distributed had stood talking to her in one corner. True, the entire population of Hedges had been watching them, as many as could crowd into the tiny room, at least, but that had not mattered.

"When are you leaving, Bob?" she had asked him.

"Tonight for sure," he had answered. After that there had been a long pause.

"And you won't be back—for a long time?"

"I must make money, Marian, and how's a fellow to do it in this town? There are enough here now; they never get anywhere, just work, eat, and sleep. I don't see how they can stand it! But I'll be back in a few years."

"But do you feel sure of making money in the city? Mr. Crane wants you to work in his store, and it would be just a little while—"

"Oh, spuds, I'd deliver groceries the rest of my life and never get any farther! No, it's a dead cinch I can do better'n that in the city!" And then had followed another long pause.

"Will you always care—a lot?" she had finally asked.

"Of course I will, it could be no other way, Marian. A man never forgets—"

"Here, take this. It just came this morning, and don't ever, ever forget! And, and—good-bye." And thrusting the locket into his bewildered, outstretched hand, she had run from the building, forgetting her mail.

Someone had snickered. At the recollection he had a sudden vision of how amusing he must have appeared, standing there holding the locket, blushing perhaps. But the snickering had jerked him back to reality; a very confused reality. In a heat of perplexity he, too, had dashed through the door without his mail.

And all that seemed to be years and years ago!

He picked up a telegram from the bed on which he was sitting, and the words seemed to shout themselves from the written page: "Marian died this morning. Pneumonia. Please come." He laid the message down, and again gazed 'at the locket, bewilderment and confusion written on his face. Of course he could come, but why, now that it was all over?

It seemed to him, now, as he sat on the edge of the bed moodily staring out of the window, that he had been indifferently listening to a concert. And it must have been beautiful, for now that the music had ceased and the musicians and patrons departed the concert hall had grown suddenly dull and cold. Nor did he have the power to call them back again. Could he gain anything by going after them? . . . Perhaps he did not visualize the concert hall, nor the musicians and patrons, but he did feel that the song and dance were over. No, he would not go back.

It wasn't a large room, and it faced a side alley. Directly out of his window he could see the dull brick wall of Crantz's "New and Slightly

Used Haberdashery," with the added information, "The Working-man's Friend," painted in staggered white letters upon a purple back-ground. There were duller streaks marked grotesquely by rain-water that had dripped from the clogged drain-pipe; and there were also many green lichen stains, for the air was damp with the breath of the bay that lay just a short way off.

The bed on which the man sat was a straggling bit of furniture, as were most of the articles in the room. It was a room one might find in any lodging-house along the water-front of any coast city. The air was damp, for it had rained all the morning, and the fog still clung stickily to the ground and buildings.

Bob was foreman now of a long-shoreman gang, and made good wages. He could have "gone back" months before. Yes, he should have gone back to her long before this. He had been away for years. Now she was dead, and someone at her death-bed had asked him to come, perhaps at her request. Was it fitting that he should go after all this waiting? It is doubtful if he was conscious of all the mental reasoning occurring in his mind. There are times when the mind becomes an organism apart, and through sheer lack of guidance maintains its own equilibrium.

It was a long time before he was certain of a definite purpose. He wasn't sure that he had been searching for a fixed plan. He wouldn't go back. It was needless. No one really cared. The telegram was merely the fulfillment of a last request. And so what did it matter? There were none to tell him how he should live, and none who cared how he acted in a crisis of this sort. His dream was ended; he must make for himself a new dream. He would go away, severing all con-tacts with those who had known him; after that, life would work itself out.

The fog lifted for a moment, but the night slipped in to take its place.

II

There was a little rustic bench about fifty yards back from the water's edge. A tiny stream tumbled past it, struggled for a minute across a short stretch of sand, then slid off into the silvery heaving breast of the ocean. The moon slipped from cloud to cloud, throwing the land into shifting reliefs of black and white. The air was warm with the balm of June—warmth and gentleness indescribable. Except for an occasional long-drawn sob, rising to a full-voiced climax, and then fading into a faintly heard sigh from the restive waters, there was silence—the age-old voice of pensiveness. It was a silence that seemed to lift one from the commonalty of fact and existence into silent communication with the stars.

Seated on the bench at the foot of a great shadowy tree was a young couple. When they spoke at all it was in the barest whisper. They seemed more absorbed in the utter peacefulness of things than the mere exchange of words.

"Wouldn't it be wonderful if the moments like this could live on forever—without end—!"

"Oh, but they do, my dear girl, in a man's memory. That is one thing that you can never destroy—the recollections of things beautiful. That, I believe, is the creed of the living—to remember!"

The two were silent after this. His arm slipped down around her shoulders, she drew closer and relaxed, calmly happy. Presently, from somewhere in the rear of the two, came drifting the muffled strains of music, a slowly swinging waltz. The girl laughed softly.

"I wonder if they have missed us yet; if they will wonder where we have gone?"

"Let them bother. This will be our last night together for some time."

"Oh, are you leaving! I didn't know that."

"I didn't either, until this afternoon. I have been waiting in dread for it to happen, though—a European representative to visit the firm, you see."

"That will be lovely. But when will you be back to Manor-on-the-Height, Lon? It must be soon!"

"It will be soon, very soon."

Again there was silence—and the boom of the breathing water. The music could only be heard at long intervals, when the scarcely moving breeze from the vast ocean would cease altogether for a brief moment. She reached up and was fumbling with his watch-chain, pulling at it coquettishly. But suddenly growing more serious, and giving him an appealing look, she exclaimed:

"Lon, I hope our love will be as eternal as those stars up there!"

"It will be, dear!"

As though perfectly certain that her prayer would be answered even as he predicted she resumed her play with his chain. Presently she asked:

"Why do you love me?"

The man didn't answer for a strained minute. "That is a hard question to answer. I don't know just how to answer it. It's not for your physical qualities alone, and they are so many. Does anyone know why he loves another person?"

"I should think he would. But you *do,* don't you? Love me, I mean."

"Yes, of course."

At this last answer she gave his watch-chain a rather hard tug pulling one end of it out of his pocket.

"Oh, see what I've done. Excuse me please! My, what an odd piece you have for your chain! What is it? There's something written on the back. I can't make it out. Where did you get it? If I may ask."

"It's just a piece of tin, it really has no meaning," and he made to put it back in his pocket.

"May I see it, please? The writing, though, I can't make it out. What does it say?"

"Do you really want to know?"

"Yes—No, I'm just curious, is all. Don't bother. I'll put it back."

"It might make a difference—I should, though."

"How you are talking! Why should you? What is it?"

"Promise me—never mind. This is the writing: 'All the love in the world,' and 'M.L.' Marian Lockwood's initials."

"Marian Lockwood! Who was she?"

"A girl I once knew."

"And you loved *her?* Tell me!"

"I hardly know."

"You hardly—Oh, Lon, speak to me. Tell me. You loved her?" She was watching his face eagerly.

"That was so long ago. . . . How can I say!"

"Then you *don't* know for sure if you love me?"

"Oh, I do! Yes, Dear Girl!"

She sat staring at him, and under the sharpness of her eyes a strange, haunting confusion overtook him. He glanced away. He tried to talk, to tell her Marian Lockwood was dead, that it had only been youthful infatuation. But he couldn't. It seemed such a useless thing to do. She was speaking softly:

"No, Lon, I'm afraid of you. I could never be sure, you see. One ought to be sure at a time like this, don't you think? Come, let us go in now. How chilly it is. Oh, look, the moon has come out. . . . Perhaps it was just the moon, after all . . . !" Without waiting for him she started off.

The man stood for a moment watching the water come and go with a certain rhythm; an uncertain rhythm. There was a look of bewilderment in his eyes. He turned and spoke quickly:

"Alice—"

The girl had already stepped across the tiny tumbling stream, and was ascending a trail into the night.

III

It was a large room, and the deep shadows made it appear even larger. The shades were pulled and any faint light that might have crept in was absorbed by thick rugs and tapestries. A low light burned at a little table covered with papers.

The air was heavy with the odor of medicines. A nurse leaned over the side of an immense canopied bed, as though listening to the breathing of the quiet form that occupied it. Another nurse talked in low, earnest tones to three doctors who had gathered close to the little table. As she talked she would occasionally point to the papers, or pick them up, and glance through them. There was a feeling of expectancy, and of patient waiting.

Children's voices shrill with laughter were heard very faintly. The rumble of a dray sounded far off.

The figure in the bed moved slightly: his hands moving across his breast to his neck. His limbs became tense after that. The nurse caught her breath and looked more closely at the blanched face, then moving quickly toward the group of doctors. They appeared to be waiting for her, and at her whispered words nodded knowingly.

One of the trio walked to the bedside, and bent down to the lips. He pulled the covers back to straighten out the arms, and found one hand tightly clenched about a small object, as though the dying man had clutched it with his last conscious strength. With a slight wrench the fingers were pulled apart, and a tiny silver locket was disclosed. A silver trinket neatly made, but not at all extraordinary. It was nothing to compel a second glance.

The doctor removed the locket from the man's neck, where it hung by a frail chain. He examined it hastily, and found it to be worn smooth on either side.

"What is it?" asked the nurse at his elbow.

"Oh, just piece of tin. Rather old, I fancy." Laying the locket on the service-table by the head of the bed, he pulled the sheets over the body, and glanced at his watch.

Notes

Introduction

1. Notes for "En roulant ma boule, roulant . . . ," McNickle Collection, The Newberry Library, Chicago. The McNickle Collection is as yet uncataloged.

2. Application materials sent to John Collier, Commissioner of Indian Affairs, 4 May 1934, McNickle Collection, The Newberry Library.

3. Louis Riel (1844–1885) led the two Métis uprisings (1870 and 1885) against the Canadian government. After the first Riel Rebellion, the Canadian government had promised to honor aboriginal land titles; when it failed to do so, Riel led the second revolution. The Métis uprisings were also caused by economic and social discrimination against the Métis. In 1885 Riel was executed, and his supporters fled across the Canadian-American border into Montana. For a discussion of Métis history and culture, see Jacqueline Peterson and Jennifer S.H. Brown, eds., *The New Peoples: Being and Becoming Métis in North America* (University of Manitoba Press, 1985). See also Marcel Giraud, *Le Métis Canadien: son rôle dans l'Histoire des provinces le l'ouest* (1945), translated as *The Métis in the Canadian West* by George Woodcock (University of Nebraska Press, 1986).

4. Ruth was born in 1900 and Florence in 1901. Dorothy Parker makes a case in her biography of D'Arcy McNickle (University of Nebraska Press, forthcoming) that William McNickle initiated the enrollment of Philomene and the children as a way of acquiring land for himself.

5. Manuscript version of *The Surrounded*, McNickle Collection. The manuscript is neither titled nor dated, but McNickle's diaries and correspondence suggest that this is an early version of *The Surrounded*, called "The Hungry Generations."

6. Letter from D'Arcy McNickle to Karen C. Fenton, 15 October 1974, McNickle Collection.

7. Letter from Mrs. Gus Dahlberg (Philomene Parenteau) to the Commissioner of Indian Affairs, 27 October 1914, McNickle Collection.

8. Harold E. Fey and D'Arcy McNickle, *Indians and Other Americans: Two Ways of Life Meet* (1959; New York and Evanston: Harper and Row, 1970), 129.

9. McNickle used the name D'Arcy Dahlberg during his time at the University of Montana. His fiction and poems published in the *Frontier*, the university's literary journal, appeared under that name.

10. Diary, 11 August 1932, McNickle Collection.

11. McNickle outlined his employment history in his letter of application to John Collier, 4 May 1934, McNickle Collection.

12. Diary, 19 January 1932, McNickle Collection.

13. Letter from D'Arcy McNickle to Professor William Gates, 25 March 1934, McNickle Collection.

14. Application material sent to John Collier, Commissioner of Indian Affairs, 4 May 1934, McNickle Collection.

15. Alfonso Ortiz, "D'Arcy McNickle (1904–1977): 'Across the River and Up the Hill'—A Personal Reminiscence," *Wassaja* 6, No. 1, (1978): 12–13.

16. Draft of the letter of application to John Collier, Commissioner of Indian Affairs, 4 May 1934, McNickle Collection.

17. Letter from D'Arcy McNickle to Professor Richard Pope, 15 March 1975, McNickle Collection.

Two collections of Salish trickster stories are available: *Salish Coyote Stories* (Salish Flathead Culture Committee of the Confederated Salish and Kootenai Tribes, 1981) and *Stories from Our Elders* (Flathead Culture Committee, 1979). Studies on the trickster figure in oral traditions can be found in Paula Gunn Allen, ed., *Studies in American Indian Literature: Critical Essays and Course Designs* (Modern Language Association, 1983); Barbara Babcock, "'A Tolerated Margin of Mess': The Trickster and His Tales Reconsidered," *Journal of the Folklore Institute* 11 (1975), 147–86; Paul Radin, *The Trickster: A Study in American Indian Mythology* (1948; New York: Schocken, 1972); Bo Scholer, ed., *Coyote Was Here: Essays on Contemporary Native American Literary and Political Mobilization*, (The Dolphin No. 9, 1984); Mourning Dove, *Coyote Stories*, ed. Heister Dean Guie, with notes by L. V. McWhorter

(1933: Univ. of Nebraska Press, 1990; introduction and notes to the Bison Book ed. by Jay Miller); Mac Linscott Ricketts, "The North American Indian Trickster," *The History of Religions* 5 (1966), 327–50; and Andrew Wiget, "His Life in His Tail: The Native American Trickster and the Literature of Possibility," in *Redefining American Literary History*, ed. A. LaVonne Brown Ruoff and Jerry W. Ward, Jr. (Modern Language Association, 1991), 83–96.

18. See, for example, Momaday, *House Made of Dawn* (1968); Silko, *Storyteller* (1981); Vizenor, *Wordarrows* (1978); Welch, *Winter in the Blood* (1974); Erdrich, *Love Medicine* (1984).

19. See, for example, Oskison, *Brothers Three* (1935) and Mathews, *Sundown* (1934).

THE RESERVATION

"Hard Riding"

McNickle's unpublished short stories were collected in Birgit Hans, ed., "The Hawk Is Hungry: An Annotated Anthology of D'Arcy McNickle's Short Fiction," (M.A. Thesis, University of Arizona, 1986). The thesis contains some detailed textual discussions of the stories' different versions. "Hard Riding" was subsequently published in Bernd C. Peyer, ed., *The Singing Spirit: Early Short Stories by North American Indians* (Tucson: University of Arizona Press, 1989).

McNickle often created fictional tribes, such as the Mountain Indians and the Little Elk Tribe in *Wind from an Enemy Sky;* he seems to employ fictional tribes to signal the didactic nature of some of his writing.

"En roulant ma boule, roulant . . ."

The only complete version of "En roulant ma boule, roulant . . ." is handwritten and probably a fragment. The last paragraph of the holograph, omitted here, sets the scene at Le Premier's house for an encounter between the tribal patriarch and Dieudonné. Brackets in the text as well as in other short stories indicate those words whose meaning I could only guess or not determine at all.

McNickle mentions a number of French explorers who made significant contributions in the settling of Canada, especially of the Three Rivers (Trois Rivières) and Quebec areas: Jean de Biencourt Poutrincourt (1557–1615), Sieur de Pontgrave (latter half of the 16th century but probably died first half of the 17th), Samuel de Champlain (c. 1567–1635); Pierre Esprit Radisson (1636–c. 1710), Medart Chouart Groseilliers (1625–1684), Pierre de Troyes

(?–1687), and Pierre Le Moyne d'Iberville (1661–1706). The brothers-in-law Groseilliers and Radisson did not only undertake several expeditions into the still unknown West but were also instrumental in founding the Hudson Bay Company while briefly, though repeatedly, serving the British. D'Iberville is frequently called the "first great Canadian"; in his later years he established the first settlement in Louisiana in the Gulf of Mexico (*Appletons' Cyclopedia of American Biography* [New York: D. Appleton and Company, 1896] and Dumas Malone, ed., *Dictionary of American Biography* [New York: Charles Scribner's Sons, 1932]).

At the beginning of "En roulant ma boule, roulant . . ." McNickle describes the judges as struggling with different legal systems—English common law, the Napoleonic Code, statutory law, Blackstone and Chancellor Kent—which they do not understand. William Blackstone (1723–1780) was the first to explain English common law in his *Commentaries on the Laws of England* (1765–1769). James Kent (1763–1847), in turn, used Blackstone's work for his explorations of American common law after the Revolution. Kent's *Commentaries on American Law* (1826, 1830) offered the first comprehensive treatment of American law and remained a standard work until the end of the 19th century. The Napoleonic Code (1804) refers to the revision of French civil laws by Napoleon I. The Napoleonic Code was used in the French-ruled territories, e.g., province of Quebec and Louisiana Territory (*The Guide to American Law* [St. Paul, et al.: West Publishing Company, 1989]).

"Meat for God"

Published in *Esquire* (September 1935), 86, 120, 122. Sam Peël, the main character in "Meat for God," traces his ancestry to Pierre Le Moyne d'Iberville (1661–1706), the "first great Canadian," who subsequently began the French settlement of Louisiana. Interestingly, Sam Peël's outward appearance does not distinguish him from the full-blood Indians and he himself barely remembers that he is a white man. McNickle's nonjudgmental description of Sam Peël illustrates the French custom of encouraging marriages between fur trappers and Indian women. The British settlers, on the other hand, did not advocate intermarriage.

McNickle also refers to a crucial period of Flathead (Salish) history in "Meat for God": the coming of the Jesuit missionaries, mere harbingers of other settlers. Sam Peël calls his life-long friend and father-in-law Big Ignace. From 1831 to 1839 the Flathead sent four delegations to St. Louis to request the services of the Black Robes, the Jesuit missionaries. The Flathead had received rudimentary instructions in the Catholic faith from some Catholic Iroquois, among them one called Ignace, who had moved into Flathead territory from Caughnawaga Mission near Sault Ste. Louis. White trappers, living among the Flathead much like Sam Peël in "Meat for God," also furthered the Flathead's interest in Catholicism. The most important reason for the Flathead to seek out the Jesuits may have been their belief that they could gain the Black Robes' supernatural powers, thereby attaining an advantage over their traditional enemies, the Blackfeet and the Sioux.

The 1831 delegation reached St. Louis but could not gain a commitment from the Jesuits to send missionaries. In 1835 Ignatius Francis or Ignace La Moose, called Old Ignace, went to St. Louis with his two young sons, but he could not exact a promise from the church either. Two years later, in 1837, Old Ignace led another delegation; however, all Flathead were killed by Sioux before reaching their goal. Two young Iroquois, one of them named Ignace Chapped Lips or Young Ignace, undertook the final journey in a quest for the Black Robes in 1839. The following year Father Peter John de Smet made his first visit to the Flathead territory; the year after that the first permanent mission was built. (John Fahey, *The Flathead Indians* [Norman: University of Oklahoma Press, 1974], 64–70; Claude Schaeffer, "The First Jesuit Mission to the Flathead, 1840–1850: A Study in Culture Conflict" [*Pacific Northwest Quarterly*, Vol. 28, 1937], 227–50).

"Snowfall"
Published in *Common Ground* 4, No. 4 (1944), 75–82. McNickle uses a fictional reservation, Two Buttes Reservation; interestingly enough, the story's three earlier versions are set in the same fictional setting as *Wind from an Enemy Sky*, the Little Elk Reservation. Henry Jim's death and his last wish also echo McNickle's posthumously published novel.

"Train Time"
Published in *Indians at Work* (1936). Children and adults in "Train Time" are merely identified as Indians; however, the severe winter and the French names indicate a northern setting.

MONTANA
"The Hawk Is Hungry"
The McNickle Collection at The Newberry Library contains four distinct versions of "The Hawk Is Hungry." McNickle experienced some problems in

determining who could narrate the death of the brown hen Molly most effectively.

"Debt of Gratitude"

There are two incomplete earlier versions of "Debt of Gratitude" in the McNickle Collection; they experiment with the story's narrative frame.

"The Wedding Night"

The version of "The Wedding Night" included in this collection is the only one in the McNickle Collection.

"Newcomers"

"Newcomers" underwent very little editing in its three extant versions. McNickle merely shifted the focus from East/West marriages to East/West democratic ideals.

"Man's Work"

Apart from a brief outline of the story in a diary entry, this heavily edited version is the only one in the McNickle Collection.

"Going to School"

Published in the *Frontier* 9 (Nov. 1928 to May 1929), 339–46) under the name D'Arcy Dahlberg.

THE CITY

"Manhattan Wedlock"

The McNickle Collection includes three versions of "Manhattan Wedlock" which show minimal editing.

"Let the War Be Fought"

This is the only complete version of "Let the War Be Fought" in the possession of The Newberry Library.

"In the Alien Corn"

"In the Alien Corn" was originally a part of "The Hungry Generations," an earlier manuscript version of *The Surrounded.*

"Six Beautiful in Paris"

The handwritten version included in this collection is probably a fragment.

"The Silver Locket"

Published in the *Frontier* 4 (Nov. 1923), 18–21, under the name D'Arcy Dahlberg.

ABOUT THE EDITOR

BIRGIT HANS was born and raised in Germany. In 1988 she received a Ph.D. in English from the University of Arizona. She is an assistant professor in Indian Studies at the University of North Dakota. She has published several articles on D'Arcy McNickle among others.